Unsafe Attachments

By the same author

Dumped! A Single Mother Shoots From the Hip

Unsafe Attachments

Caroline Oulton

HUTCHINSON

LONDON

Published by Hutchinson 2008

2 4 6 8 10 9 7 5 3 1

Copyright © Caroline Oulton 2008

Caroline Oulton has asserted her right under the Copyright, Designs
and Patents Act 1988 to be identified as the author of this work

This is a work of fiction. Names and characters are the product of the author's
imagination and any resemblance to actual persons, living or dead,
is entirely coincidental.

The author and publisher would like to thank the following for permission to
use copyright material:

'Those Three Days' Words & Music by Lucinda Williams © Warner-Tamerlane
Publishing Corp and Lucy Jones Music. All rights administered by
Warner/Chappell Music Ltd, London W6 8BS. Reproduced by permission.

'Walk the Jetty' Words & Music by Eileen Rose © Eileen Rose.
Reproduced by permission.

First published in Great Britain in 2008 by
Hutchinson
Random House, 20 Vauxhall Bridge Road,
London SW1V 2SA

www.rbooks.co.uk

Addresses for companies within The Random House Group Limited can be
found at: www.randomhouse.co.uk/offices.htm

The Random House Group Limited Reg. No. 954009

A CIP catalogue record for this book
is available from the British Library

ISBN 9780091921095

The Random House Group Limited supports The Forest Stewardship Council
(FSC), the leading international forest certification organisation. All our titles
that are printed on Greenpeace approved FSC certified paper carry the FSC
logo. Our paper procurement policy can be found at:
www.rbooks.co.uk/environment

Mixed Sources
Product group from well-managed
forests and other controlled sources
www.fsc.org Cert no. TT-COC-2139
© 1996 Forest Stewardship Council
FSC

Typeset by SX Composing DTP, Rayleigh, Essex
Printed and bound in Great Britain by
CPI Mackays, Chatham, ME5 8TD

For Moops and Carrie
Lodestars

Acknowledgements

Heartfelt thanks are due to Marcus Adams, Sharon Chin, Kate Fawkes, Helen Greaves, Tatiana Kennedy, Phyllida Lloyd, Caroline Miller Smith, Phyl Newall, Derek Oulton, Harry Oulton, Jane Turnbull and Jo Willett for their sterling generosity in scooping up endless tabs . . .

Contents

'A crude invitation, a little libation, to jump start something. Come on . . . Shake the sand off, walk the jetty with me, toss your line out . . . Hey, you might as well . . .'

Eileen Rose, 'Walk the Jetty', from the album *Shine Like It Does*

'Did you love me forever
just for those three days . . .'

Lucinda Williams, 'Those Three Days', from the album *World Without Tears*

Foreword
(The Way It Is Sometimes . . .)

O N A SUMMER evening, if you stand still and listen, you can hear the whole honeycomb of the city ticking and humming with infidelity. Lovers' thoughts ripple through the air like tiny birds and bounce off your skin. Call them in and blush. Pause for a moment to decipher discreet gestures or half-smiles. Everyone's emotional charts are cross-hatched with deceit, and little lights wink as people make connections. There is so much these days that you can get away with, and this is the map.

It's close of play in mid-June at around six-thirty as people pour down the main drag shrugging off their working fatigue to step out lightly for home. Singletons pause to pick up luscious oddments for their suppers. Strides lengthen and chins tilt. It's warmer than it has been; enticing bits of girl peep out of brightly coloured wrappings, and breasts and lips seem on offer once again. Hooray. It's that exciting moment in the day, when, for people suspended momentarily between their professional and domestic zones, a kiss, a dare, a lie dangles just within reach . . .

And at exactly that moment, a professional woman swinging past a zinc-clad bar spies a clutch of junior sprats. It's important for morale, she thinks, for them to see me off-piste, and maybe, just for once, it might be quite fun. My husband can deal with the kids. Why not? And how I'd like that wine, just the one cold glass, in my fuchsia silk shirt with my love-that-pink lipstick and my tight black skirt slashed up the side. I'm a serious solicitor, seriously sexy, and I'll sip some fine wine with those smart lawyer boys outside at that wobbly table, I don't mind if I do. As she stretches out her legs to admire her ankles it starts to rain, and, tipping back her head, she opens her mouth and laughs. One of the boys, noticing that her throat is beautiful, holds a jacket over her head and puts his arm round her, easing her inside. Briefly, her face gets pushed against his neck. He smells, to her, unbearably young, and suddenly, there in the doorway, she wants to cry.

A few streets away the warm rain streams down slanting glass panes, high up in a square, high above the trees. The window frames are matte, metal, industrial, forged in the twenties and probably listed. An architect shuts the windows with a special pole and adjusts the tiny figures in his bold new model of a bold new building, watched by a glossy assistant. She is Colombian, achingly gifted, and asks for his help with her own little project. It seems a bit late to be starting this now, but hey, she has a boyfriend who is slightly depressed and he has a wife whom he's had for some time. And so the architect gently lifts her elbow off the drawing board to inspect a detail. Well, that's how it starts and no one is remotely surprised. In fact, her brother cheats, too, on his very young wife. She has twins, misses her family and wants to go home. He washes up in a basement. He has holes in his shoes, and when it rains his feet get soggy as the door is badly fitted. God knows he must have something to look forward to.

A journalist, who buys croissants from the café above that basement, cracks his knuckles as he consults his watch. He knows that his boyfriend will be working late. He should go home now, even so, to be there for when his lover does get back, ground down by stress and as fractious and jumpy as a cross little cat. Yes, the journalist knows he should return to their bare-wood, pared-back dinky Georgian house, but somehow, tired as he is, attached to his partner as he is, he doesn't. Forcing open a tiny frosted window in the toilet at work, he feels a sparkle in the air. Red brake lights beckon. It's stopped raining and the streets glisten up at him, shiny black and lickable. Come out and play. Yes, you, now, before it gets dark. There could be someone waiting and your cheeky pint-sized lover won't be back for hours. Quickly drying his hands he slips back into reception, and, as he'd half expected, the foxy young salesman is still fiddling about with his briefcase and pens. 'There's quite a nice pub just round the corner . . .'

The moment their lips touch the foam, a girl rolls over on her bed in a designer hotel across the way. She slaps petulantly at the side table for her funky little watch. She'd taken it off before sex, would have felt silly wearing only that, a bit like men and socks. He's squatting naked at the minibar and has lovely hands.

'Drink, sweetie?'

'No way,' she says. 'I really have to go.'

The man smiles at her and puts his finger to his lips. 'Sssshhhhh,' he says. 'You can't go now.'

'Why not?' she asks crossly, already halfway back into her other drabber life, the one she spends too much time in, far away across town. She pushes her feet hard into expensive shoes.

'You mustn't go, my darling.' He stands up and reaches out to touch her oh, so gently with the cold beer can in his hand. 'You can't go now because it's raining and you're much too pretty to get wet. Listen. Just for a moment.'

It's raining again all over town. People wait, take a breath and imagine anything is possible as the summer dusk slides in, hiding faces and fuelling illicit dreams.

Arrival

THE MAUVE summer night sky and airport lights intoxicated the children and they started to emit competitive high-pitched mouse squeaks, racking up the frequency as their mother bucked the buggy over another kerb. She squinted at a tiny suspended screen. *Baggage in hall.* Does that mean kids, wife or both? She snorted loudly at the thought, startling passers-by.

Earlier that evening, watching her daughter peel toasted cheese off slices of toast and discard both in messy heaps, Dinah wondered why she lacked the energy to remonstrate. Eventually, scrolling tiredly back through her never-ending day, she remembered. Deep into her sleep tunnel that morning, she'd sensed the baby muttering and harrumphing about, and in response had lashed herself away from the moment of waking, fleeing the chatter as it turned into squawks. When the squawks had morphed into train-whistle screams, reluctantly Dinah had unglued her eyes. The action had seemed to take the same amount of effort as heaving up heavy garage doors. 'Joules' flew into her head, a word she hadn't needed since school. Then she had screamed herself. Black swimming goggles were bobbing about two inches from her face, blocking her view of the room. Otherwise the little boy was naked, apart from his flippers. He had crawled over her, twisting his head sideways through the open window, prior to climbing out. As she retrieved him wearily, Dinah noticed a bright blue sheet carefully spread out on the paving stones two storeys below her.

'Divin',' he'd said laconically.

Sensitive to scents just now, she was sure that she'd shut her window before she went to sleep, demented by an ugly male cologne several gardens away. But then she also remembered wrenching it open again in the small hours in a fit of night sweats. Fortunately it had jammed a few inches up and she had rolled back to sleep, defeated. All through that subsequent endless day she had been plagued by involuntary flashes, her son in an aerial snapshot, smashed up on the bloody blue sheet.

The rejected cheese and bread was sliding about in water from up-ended beakers as Dinah pulled herself together.

'I know, we'll go and meet Daddy. That'll be fun, won't it?'

It was an unlikely initiative, but it gave her a much needed jolt of adrenalin and Heathrow yielded only one possible flight. With the kitchen glossed over and the children abruptly mopped and pyjama-ed, Dinah's hysterically anticipated soak doze was immediately interrupted by the toddler. She peered crossly over the bath rim trying to pull off her mother's nipple, assuming it was a button or some other detachable object.

Several streets away Mel was fiddling about trying on different bangles. She had packed her small son off early for a sleepover as she found him invasive when she wanted to titivate. Tiny, with absurdly long dead-straight hair, Mel lived with her boyfriend, who worked in the Far East and was rarely around. He was easy-going, owned the house, and, coming as he did from a shambolic, close-knit family, loved Mel and her child without thinking about it over much.

Hauling herself out of the bath, Dinah bought herself another few moments of relative quiet by giving her toddler the toothpaste to play with. She tried to think where there might be some clean underwear, and, scrabbling around, encountered a scruffy old nursing bra scrunched at the back of a drawer. She grinned as she scooped it out, amused that her husband had been intrigued by the mechanisms of the different models: assorted combinations of zips, hooks and velcro. Did milk spurt out when you came, like in that painting of Venus? Hard to say. Dinah remembered having to sleep in her maternity bra stuffed out with layers of sogging breast pads to avoid leakage. Not sexy. Discarding the voluminous greyish bra, she smiled again as she basked in a fantasy of an alternative self larking about having golden afternoon sex with her husband while the babies slept and milk shot out of her breasts as she climaxed!

Shit, shit, shit. The toddler, incensed by her inability to open the toothpaste, had bitten into the side of it and was rubbing bright blue gel into her hair. 'She thinks it's shampoo,' jeered her brother, getting referred pleasure from the mess and sensation, even though he was likely to field at least some of the screeching maternal fall-out.

Mel was meticulously flossing her teeth. She had foxy little incisors, not her best feature, so she focused instead on her secondary undercover relationship, which had been progressing nicely for just under a year now. The man, an academic, was highly thought-of in his field, and she was starting to make waves in a related one. Having had their eyes on each other for some time, they had slipped into bed easily enough via a lift at a conference. On the rare occasions that Mel remembered the man's wife and two veg, her mind slid over them as featureless mounds. She had few details to snag on as she knew almost nothing about them, and that way they remained beige and inconsequential.

The man never specifically said that his relationship with his wife had run its course, but he implied it and often seemed tired. Mel was certain they never had sex any more. Well . . . possibly the odd duty exchange after a long day, but not in a million years the sweaty, screaming engulfment into which she and he routinely descended. Inconceivable. It was probably his wife who had insisted on having the children in the first place, and with her tacky, lowbrow job hadn't a hope of understanding the man's brilliance. It just wouldn't be possible for his wife to scoot about provocatively amongst his academic hobby horses in the way that she, Mel, did, during exotic lunches of home-baked bread, no underwear, and caper berries. She usually remembered to be generous about her female colleagues, sensing, rightly, that it made her more attractive. Then she would confuse and arouse her lover with the breadth of her sexual demands, having recently added scratching and biting to her repertoire. She wanted to mark the man out as hers. He, for his part, felt unable to explain that it caused him difficulties in the bathroom or on family holidays, although so far he'd managed to conceal all of this from his wife, who seemed amused by his new-found enthusiasm for white T-shirts in bed, American-style. The man rarely got away in the evenings because of his family commitments, but Mel felt more relaxed during the day anyway, when her porcine son was at school. Then there was no risk of his hanging around her lover and unnerving him. The child didn't fit properly into anyone's picture, and he sensed it and it made him worse.

Mel was confused by what exactly it was that she

wanted at the moment. She had lost interest in her child's father pretty swiftly, and even though her current partner loved her, she seemed to have moved from fantasising about marrying him to wanting her new lover's own marriage officially sundered. Why, she couldn't say, as the arrangement as it stood suited her fine and she felt no guilt about the wife. Quite clearly the man wouldn't be happy to devote so much time to her if he rated his existing family.

Hurling her children into their car seats, Dinah peeled a tattered Teletubby magazine that her daughter sometimes favoured off the floor. There were melted chocolate buttons stuck to one of the pages which the supperless little girl might discover en route. Being subjected to a low-blood-sugar tantrum didn't bear thinking about; and Dinah always had nasty near-misses twisting round to quell her. She must remember to throw away the magazine at the airport, though, as her husband would be massively disapproving. Once, Dinah remembered, swerving, he'd inadvertently ripped the paper eyes off a brightly coloured plastic truck, intent on removing every last pasted-on ad for petrol or cereal. Why was this van backing up on her now? Logos on clothes, television programmes, junk food – he tried to shield his children from it all. Dinah wasn't unsympathetic, but at times it did seem a Sisyphean battle.

A young couple tripped out of a café, airily crossing

too close to the car. The girl was pretty with plum lipstick and looked at Dinah without seeing her. These days cafés seemed an unattainable luxury, and Dinah fretted that she had never accorded them enough attention when she'd had the chance. People wrote postcards in them, flirted in them, kissed in them; principally young people and foreigners, it must be said, but even so. There was one in North London called Solace, a perfect café name, and when she drove past it with carloads of screaming children, its invitingly creamy façade seemed to mock her for having missed her chance. The traffic was certainly sluggish. Dinah glanced at her watch, unable, suddenly, to remember how many minutes slow it was. Unless the plane was delayed she would be hard pushed to park, decant the kids and hurtle to Arrivals in time.

'Yook phlowhas,' screeched the toddler. Dinah peered down a side street and by changing lanes could just make out dying flowers tied to nearby railings and bedraggled in the gutter. It reminded her of Lady Di's death and the tidal wave of bouquets encased in soggy cellophane and all smeary with condensation in that park.

'Bear,' yelped her daughter insistently. 'Bear, bear, bear.'

She had spotted a fluorescent pink teddy left near the flowers with a note. Someone must have died. Dimly Dinah remembered a photograph on the front of the *Kilburn Times*: two badly smashed-up cars, joyriders probably, and hadn't there been a child involved? That might explain the teddy. She struggled to piece together the details that were floating about on the edge of her memory, mushing into the accident that morning that her son hadn't actually had. How horrid. It clouded her thoughts for a while. Then the traffic eased, and Dinah, conscious of her own prurience and the widening gap in front of her, hastily jumped the car forward. Where was she going? Thankfully Heathrow was in the same general direction as her job, towards which she now realised she'd been driving on autopilot.

Shying away from death and mourning, Dinah remembered, relieved, that she hadn't quite exhausted her nursing bra train of thought in connection with her husband. For someone so supremely self-centred, he did have the oddest tics. Soiled nappies, for example, couldn't be put in municipal bins in case a tramp encountered them rummaging for scraps of food. Even though she dismissed this prohibition as absurd, Dinah had been unable to rid herself ever since of the frightening image of a homeless person with a hand and possibly beard smeared with her baby's faeces. Her husband had been surprisingly good, though, over her evening fits of despair. When Dinah, ratty with the endless sucking and the flicker of mastitis, had yelled at him to go and get bottles and formula, he would come back breezily with a four pack of Guinness and suggest holding out for just one more day. Against all the odds, whichever baby it was would then suddenly pass out. He must somehow have absorbed the unsubtle pressure to breastfeed for ever even while he was hooting with horror at the one and a half preparation classes she had forced him to attend. That, in turn, reminded her of the long night of the shamefully unnatural second birth when she'd been sitting attached to a drip on an uncomfortable chair while he'd snored, stretched out on the bed. He claimed he'd woken up when it got interesting. He probably had. It had all been a bit of a panic as she remembered, cord wound tightly round the baby's neck, ugly tearing and so on.

Of course there were some things she didn't know about her husband. Did he wank when he was away teaching in America? It was oddly hard to imagine. Had he ever shagged any of his students? She remembered looking out on to the pool complex when she was visiting him in Florida, pre-children of course, and being electrified by the babeage factor, the physical complacency of the alpha females strutting around in luminous swimwear sucking on small bottles of Evian. Then there was the Polish girl who rang from somewhere abroad, yelping about Dinah's first pregnancy. She had sounded completely unhinged, and Dinah's husband, wincing at the sounds pouring out of the handset, had been so open about his confusion and bewilderment that Dinah genuinely hadn't cared. Somehow it had all seemed faraway and irrelevant.

The airport car park oppressed Mel after the pale, steamy approach roads. Should she wear her jacket or not? She bobbed up and down, angling the wing mirror to try and paste the relevant glimpses into a whole. In the end she left the jacket in the car although she felt the cold and usually liked to advertise the fact. She owned loads of pretty lacy thermals, and often borrowed big men's sweaters that flopped over her wrists.

Still absurdly premature, she pottered round the Sock Shop, picked up a paper cone of chilled water that she didn't want and finally gave up the pretence and went to wait at Arrivals. Between *Landed* and *Baggage in Hall,* a large, glistening woman crashed into the barriers with a pushchair, disgorging its overcooked inhabitants. Immediately they started shoving each other and licking the floor. Mel stared at them absently, relieved that her own son was past that stage. She knew that her man was going back to America to teach a semester in the autumn and wondered if it might be fun to go with him? Perhaps she could cook up some academic pretext and leave her child here. No, she didn't want to appear a bad or uncaring mother. Maybe she could keep the house, move the boyfriend out, and after a short interval move the man in, though. How could that be achieved? It might just be possible on the grounds of not disrupting her son too much. Her boyfriend was a nice guy and he'd never been mad about the location of the house anyway. Mel had only been to America once, very briefly, and quickly drifted into a pleasant reverie involving motels, freeways and oceans in which the man featured, tanned and adoring, but her lumpen small son somehow didn't.

To her delight, the toddler, while describing frenzied ellipses, had found a discarded dustpan to tip over her brother. Sweet papers, fluff and assorted detritus were now sticking to him and he bawled in outrage as his mother rummaged for Wet Ones in the buggy. The woman looked pretty near hysteria, and Mel toyed with offering to help her but couldn't face getting manky after all the effort she'd gone to to prepare herself. She'd given herself far too long to get ready, and now felt awkwardly posed and self-conscious, a varnished statuette.

The man wasn't concentrating as he meandered through the green channel. Well, he was, but on the success of his last couple of lectures rather than the next ten minutes. He was tall and looked good, in spite of his post-flight sweat glaze, in a pale, well cut mackintosh. A thoroughgoing narcissist, he had perfected a number of techniques for keeping anything difficult or unpleasant at bay, unaware, like a lot of men, of how much he did actually love his children. Usually, his primary preoccupation was with how much valuable time they were likely to devour that he had earmarked for writing or absorbing hardcore international news.

He saw Mel posed attractively against the barrier and felt pleased, flattered, but also slightly irritated by her presumption. Smiling, she pattered forward to kiss him, but just as they engaged, two blurs screamed, 'Daddy, Daddy,' and hurled themselves at his knees. The battered double buggy and his pregnant wife were only a few yards away. Mel froze. The red rabbits on his daughter's faded baby-gro leapt out at him. His wife stared at Mel and Mel looked in amazement from the wife to the children to the man and back again. The man, shocked and unable to process anything, wondered why his son seemed quite so dirty.

Dinah felt the last few months reel out in front of her very fast in slow motion. There were the timing discrepancies that her husband had smudged and she had been too tired to pursue at the time; the fact of his mobile being switched off at lunchtime; and those marks on his back that she'd noticed in the shower some time ago and then forgotten about. Killer details had been lurking just below the surface, but she was pregnant, for Christ's sake, with two young children and a job, and stalking her husband or cross-questioning him simply hadn't occurred to her.

She sat down heavily. She'd seen Mel on television once, when she'd appeared on a television programme with her husband. In fact they'd watched it together in bed around the time that this last baby was conceived. Dinah remembered the occasion vividly, as arts programming always went out after midnight and her husband had had to wake her up for it. It was definitely her. One of those 'I'm bright but only ickle really' types.

'I bet men like her but she's bogus as fuck.'

Her husband had laughed. 'You're probably right darling.'

I bloody well was right. Bang on. Bogus as a fuck, she thought fiercely. The grimy floor swung up at her. I will not be sick and I will not cry, but I can't actually stand up. Suddenly nauseous, Dinah realised that all day she had been anticipating something bad, with those unnerving images of her broken-necked son and then the memorial flowers. Whatever the final outcome of this particular collision, her entire family was going to be badly mangled by it, of that Dinah felt absolutely sure.

Mel surreptitiously checked, but no, the woman wasn't just vast, she was pregnant, something the man had omitted to mention. That seemed strange, as Mel and he were likely to be together soon, well fairly soon, in the autumn, perhaps, in America. It was inconvenient, as well, as the pregnancy made everything more awkward to finesse. Damn her! They must have been doing it after all. Well, once, maybe. She obviously wanted this child, which was pretty irresponsible when her husband so clearly didn't love her.

The man rapidly rehearsed and discarded all the possible gambits open to him. What had got into his wife? She had never ever come to the airport before, let alone with the kids at this hour. He'd been all set to cab it over to Mel's and they had made that arrangement. Mel had overstepped the mark, but not by very much. He would have slipped back home later when his wife was bound to be asleep, with vague flight delay mutterings or not even that. Now he faced emotional turbulence in all directions of the kind he least relished. Dinah really didn't need this, he could see that, and Mel would cut up damn rusty about the pregnancy and he absolutely had to finish that article this weekend.

'Daddy, Daddy,' said the little boy, tugging at his father's mackintosh and finally forcing a reaction from one of the three frozen adults. 'Miss Schofield says a snake has two willies.'

Those Doggone Party Blues

THE BILL at Sainsbury's came to £76.32. They didn't look at each other as they dug out their chequebooks. Liz took the biro on the string, so Jane smiled optimistically at the middle-aged cashier who turned away conscious of the queue starting to back up. Reluctantly she unclipped another pen from her pocket before turning back to deal with a toddler surfing on the belt whose ineffectual father was dabbing at spilt yoghurt.

Liz picked up the heavier box of booze from habit and Jane followed her out to the car park, bashing her knees against the awkward plastic bags from which the French loaves protruded. She noted with disgust that the exertion of hefting the box on to the car bonnet stretched Liz's ancient jeans even tighter across her generous arse, green chequebook flapping out of her pocket like a cartoon tongue. Jane felt snappy and provoked for no reason. A wintry sun had slid out while they shopped and it clashed with her mood. She was wearing yesterday's clothes and needed a bath. It had seemed sensible this morning to do the shopping and then move the furniture before having a shower and changing. Now, bad-tempered and sticky, she was regretting that decision. The nuclear families in the car park grated on her and the car windscreen looked like shit as she slumped into the passenger seat.

'Why are we having this fucking party anyway?'

They were the first words she'd uttered since putting the pots of houmous that Liz had selected back on the shelves with an irrational objection. Liz, preoccupied with negotiating round other cars in the sun-dirt dazzle, didn't reply. Neither of them approved of paying for the car to be washed, but as they weren't keen on spending their weekends sloshing soapy buckets around either, the car got progressively grimier.

Ten minutes later, accelerating through a red light, Liz attempted to break the silence.

'I wonder what Jacmel will come as this evening?'

This should have induced in her girlfriend an answering eye roll or shrug, perhaps, but Jane, feet up on the dash, was having none of it. They'd been so happy when they'd first met, when any student who didn't experiment with their sexuality was deemed chicken. Liz, a mature student, had always been gay and politicised, but for Jane it had been an exhilarating leap into a brand new whirlwind of female bodies and ferociously held opinions. Liz still kept effortlessly abreast of all current affairs. It was a point of principle with her and Jane had always tried to keep up, contradict her, even, but recently she had been losing impetus and had started furtively to bin the newspapers with the denser articles unread.

They went into the house without speaking. Jane started to unpack the food in the kitchen as Liz manhandled the sofa aggressively across the floor, exposing a silt of dust, paper clips and biscuit crumbs in the dents left by the castors. The room looked dreadful, thought Jane, wandering back in. She wanted to scream and run out of the house, in spite of their joint mortgage, and never return.

Liz had circles of sweat under her arms.

'Decorations?' said Jane. 'Balloons perhaps? The walls are filthy and this house is so tacky I can't stand it any more.'

Liz, grunting with the effort of galumphing an armchair into the passage, wheezed back at her, 'We are grown women not children. The house has always looked like this and that's the third time you've said tacky today.'

It should have been fun getting ready for the party, and normally they would have opened a beer and sent each other up as they caterwauled along to some big-haired country diva. The mood was definitely hardening, though. They retreated away from each other into formality, knowing that outright disagreement was impossible. Their party was almost upon them.

Candy arrived early with some revolting-looking pizzas and got in the way, so Jane went upstairs and blasted herself in the shower. She concentrated on her appearance to distract herself from her irritation with Liz, the cat's ear infection, and Candy droning on downstairs about her unfaithful girlfriend and stressy job. Snapping on silver earrings that pinched her ear lobes, she felt relieved that one item, at least, chimed with her mood. Then she wound a dark red turban round her head, smudged on some kohl, teamed wide sailor trousers with a little vest and stomped back downstairs. She looked fantastic but still felt sour and at odds with the evening. Liz, in the interim, had put on the smart blue blazer that she always wore to parties, without fucking fail, thought Jane. Give me a break. I so wish she wouldn't. It makes her look bulky and mannish. Then she felt disloyal. Then she didn't feel disloyal. Then she put on a record and started to dance, a little eccentric with just the one guest. She had always had a strangely particular style, arms held high and crooked with her bottom thrusting out backwards. Liz looked on tolerantly. She grinned to herself, remembering her girlfriend's desirability on campus when all the men fancied her but Janey had elected to go home with Liz. On Saturdays they used to neck ostentatiously in the shopping precinct, startling buskers and horrifying shoppers, and had been together pretty much ever since. Janey was sporadically unfaithful, and a couple of years ago had run off to Rome with Sonia, who was black, sarcastic and worked in the laundrette. Liz herself had had only one other serious entanglement, a Scottish sociology teacher called Eilidh, which had lasted ten months. 'Rather mousy,' Janey had called her defensively, knowing it wasn't fair and wasn't even some of the story. Jane's dismay at this steadfast little liaison of Liz's had surprised her. Liz was immensely discreet, and if she did manage to write 'Eyelid' postcards when they were on holiday, Jane never knew about it, and she only ever rang her from work. Somehow, though, Jane had sensed that she still had the upper hand and that Liz would have given up Eilidh for her if it had come to that. Eventually Eilidh tired of being second best and switched back to male folk musicians with whom she'd always been happy before.

Liz was eating bread and pâté now, and she'd got a bit caught in her hair. Jane felt queasy and looked away. When she looked back later it had gone. Liz caught her eye and beckoned her over to dance, so Jane smiled tightly and wandered over. Okay, one dance then, can't deny her that. She even put up a pretty convincing show linking her hands behind Liz's neck and leaning back before kissing her briefly on the mouth.

The evening was long and wearisome, and Janey imagined herself looking down from the ceiling on the different groups and huddles. Blanche would undoubtedly be describing for the millionth time the strain it put on her marriage having her wastrel partner 'prime carer' for the girls. Yes, thought Jane. I can relate to that. Liz is our prime carer, even though we don't have any kids. Rose would be bored by the low-grade chit-chat and making little effort to conceal it. Jane adored American Rose with her dry humour and ungovernable hair. A struggling theatre designer, she lived two streets away in a modest flat crammed with art books, swatches of fabric and weird photos. 'A bit self-conscious,' said puritan Liz. 'Who would want to live in a stage set?' But Jane reckoned she could have handled it. Jane admired Rose's style and always flirted with her, but they had never had sex. Rose had calmly rejected her more overt advances on any number of occasions. 'Don't want to be just another of your scalps. Thanks all the same, honey.' Rose was seriously committed to her difficult and erratic girlfriend Laurie, and Jane liked her even more for that.

Jane was nowhere near as bright as Liz but always reckoned she'd do better than her in the end. 'Better by whose lights?' she imagined Liz snorting in response. A bit more money, a bit more success and, possibly, with a bit of luck, some kind of media profile. She knew she was attractive to potential employers when she bounced into their open-plan offices with her witty accessories and finely judged scorn. Gay men and smart young women were ringing her with modest commissions, she was getting better paid when she did get work, and she reckoned that at last she might be inching into more remunerative, more zeitgeisty pastures. In addition she wasn't averse to fiddling with the facts or inventing quotes to bulk out her articles. Liz worked in local government, and the battle-lines between the two of them were so achingly well drawn that they barely had the energy to bicker about their respective jobs any more.

'You'll never achieve anything significant churning out that pap.'

'Yeah, well, it's better than boring the converted day in day out.'

'Your stuff is never properly researched. You choose some vague generalisation and then invent stuff to back it up.'

'Are you telling me the radical press doesn't?'

'Your writing's mediocre, but you always put on slap and dress up before going into those offices. They're buying you.'

'Well, I like my tits and so do you, so why shouldn't they?'

And so on.

Jane had always been amused by Liz's pithy criticism of her articles, but just recently it had started to irk her. Their senses of humour and pleasure in each other seemed to be slipping out of whack. You can't wrestle with global suffering and human rights abuses every day, decided Jane. Especially as you get older.

Jane watched Liz listening patiently to IQ-of-a-plant Blanche droning on. Liz in turn smiled back across at Janey moodily propping up the door. She assumed that her partner's surliness had been accentuated by the arrival of Rose's girlfriend. Laurie was mercurial and seriously off the rails, although at the high-end florist's where she helped out, the well-heeled customers seemed thrilled by the alternating beams of exuberance and black contempt that she trained on them. Laurie did have a killer instinct for which kind of leaf, bamboo or odd berry was going to be the next thing way before it was. To amuse herself, Jane conceived a heavily illustrated piece on floral vogues, then quickly discarded it as being too middle-aged for her contacts. Laurie did a lot of drugs and occasionally picked up gruesome loser men that Liz and Jane called the rehabs. Teetering on the brink, with scars snaking up her arms, she always came back to Rose in the end, though, or between crises, depending on your viewpoint.

Jacmel's car wouldn't start. As per. God, thought Jane, striding down the drive, I'm certainly not going to help. She only has to look tearful and the whole crew'll be out there to push. I'll leave Liz the house, she thought. Yes, that'd be nice, good, generous, kind. Jane summoned positive adjectives to fight off the swarming criticisms beating melodramatic time with her footsteps. You've used her . . . sucked her dry . . . now you're bailing out . . . what will she do? Oh, for heaven's sake, stamped Jane. We'll sell the house. That's what couples who split up do. And then maybe I can buy somewhere of my own, a studio, perhaps, and make it pretty and feminine and totally unlike that dusty old albatross of a suburban monstrosity. She started selecting colours, momentarily thrown by the realisation that she only seemed able to envisage a flat identical to Rose's. I'll wear tight pastel sweaters and look out of attic windows like a French girl in a film, she decided. This fantasy was low on narrative, but it did nourish her fleetingly as she marched away from her life.

When she reached the tube it was shut, with a heavy-duty metal grille padlocked across the entrance. Wandering around the Oval past midnight would usually have made Jane edgy, but she was drunk and determined to leave home now, this minute. There were no cabs in the vicinity, but out of sheer desperation she somehow conjured up the memory of a flyblown minicab place on the next corner with ripped vinyl armchairs and a scarred counter. Slumped across the back seat, energy ebbing, she gave the cross-eyed driver her brother's address in Chiswick.

The next morning, waking up with a cracking hangover on a makeshift bed with no clean clothes, Jane didn't feel great. Her notebooks of ideas for articles, her laptop, everything she needed, in fact, was back at the house, but she couldn't return immediately. She'd ring. Yes, of course. Talk to Liz. Explain and offer to help clear up. She'd be as generous as she could, even stay over if it helped. No, perhaps she wouldn't ring, thinking about it. She'd just turn up and explain what she'd decided. She wasn't nervous, but it simply wasn't fair to do it on the phone.

Jane hopped on to the tube in a more positive mood. Surprisingly, though, when she opened the front door, feeling a bit self-conscious, she found Rose asleep on the sofa and nothing much else happening. That was weird, as Rose loved her own flat and wasn't a crashing at friends' places kind of person at all.

Jane crept upstairs, gently easing the bedroom door open. Liz swore and sat up. She was wearing Janey's favourite pink T-shirt, had smudged make-up round her eyes, and seemed seriously pissed off.

'Where did you wander off to last night? Laurie fell downstairs when everyone else had gone. We had to get her to hospital and you'd got the fucking car keys.'

'Why didn't you get a cab?'

'Saturday night. No one could come for hours, so we got an ambulance and they were hacked off as she wasn't bad enough, and then we had to walk back from the hospital.'

'Is she okay?'

'Yes, for the moment. Broke her arm. Look, I'm really shattered.'

Liz pulled the duvet back over her head. She obviously didn't get it. Jane wondered if she'd imagined wanting to leave her so badly? No, the niggling irritations would quickly get worse and erupt into much uglier scenes than this one.

Downstairs, Rose had woken up and started to potter about emptying ashtrays. Jane hovered on the stairs, unable to face her. What in God's name had been yesterday's bright idea for a safe place for her computer before the party? How could she get more clothes without disturbing Laurie, who was obviously in the other bedroom? There might be some semi-dry underwear in the airing cupboard, with any luck.

Rose spotted her through the sitting-room window as she crept away, clutching two pairs of clean knickers and her laptop. Not the most stylish exit. Feeling daunted, Jane wondered how on earth she was going to get through the rest of Sunday in manky party clothes before returning to the polite awkwardness of Chiswick.

She collected her other crucial possessions later in the week when Liz was safely at work. It was hard to believe that she had left, as nothing about the house seemed to have changed that much. Thinking about it, though, she wasn't quite sure what she'd expected. A running female outline in one of the walls as though she'd exited bodily like a cartoon cat being chased or flattened? For a few weeks, anyway, it might be best to keep a low profile. She was too proud to probe mutual friends about Liz's state of mind. Still, if Liz was okay about it, then maybe they could just have a drink or something, nothing too dramatic. When she finally rang, earlier than she had told herself she would, Liz seemed amazingly cool about everything and even suggested one of their old haunts.

Jane came swinging into the brasserie her traditional ten minutes late. She hadn't had much work recently, but hadn't wanted to suggest anywhere cheaper in case Liz guessed she was short of money. Well, Liz would be pretty lonely by now and if she seemed really insistent, Jane might go home with her, just for the night. It would be a nice gesture. But Liz didn't seem to be there. She must be in the loo or something. She never kept Jane waiting, ever, under any circumstances. That was the point. That had been the point of their relationship.

Glumly, Jane asked for a menu, ordered a drink and discreetly started looking around to distract herself from Liz's absence. Two women were perched on high stools up at the bar, oblivious to Jane's arrival at chair level, but still well within earshot. There was something intriguing about them. The smarter, taller one almost certainly worked in the City. She had glossy dark hair, great legs, and to, Janey's practised eye, a wildly expensive briefcase. Sliding off her stool, grinning, she looked at her watch.

'Don't mind if I do frankly. Those kids and that husband can do their own thing for once.'

Legs sashayed over to the loo while her companion ordered more wine. She, by contrast, wasn't remotely

Cityish. Small-boned and startlingly pretty in a fey, dishevelled kind of way, she was awash with freckles and wore a clumsy bracelet made of beach junk. Jane couldn't decide if it was deeply chic or just odd. Tiny, yacking away to the barman, didn't register her companion click-clacking back from the ladies, whereupon Legs scooped her friend's tumble of glorious reddish gold hair to one side, bent down and licked the back of her neck. Jane nearly dropped her drink. It was a long lascivious lick, absolutely no question, but they weren't lesbians. They were professional women with husbands and kids.

Baffled, Jane shook her head just as Liz strode through the doors, thinking the criticism was directed at her.

'Sorry I'm late, sweetie.'

She gave Jane a big hug and her familiar warm grin.

'Got yourself a boyfriend, then?'

They'd always joked that Jane wasn't really one hundred per cent, completely and incontrovertibly, a lesbian.

Jane shook her head as Liz looked round for the waiter.

'So how's it going? What you been up to?'

Jane smiled. 'Same old same old. How about you? You look great.'

And to Jane's surprise, Liz really did. Nothing dramatic – new dark jeans, subtle if unfamiliar scent, hair a bit longer, and maybe she'd finally lost a bit of weight, although it was hard to tell in those jeans.

They chatted warmly and easily, falling straight back into the groove. Jane needed to move out of Chiswick quite soon but hadn't found anywhere yet, and Liz's boss was giving her gyp. Jane realised that she had got quite drunk but was confident that Liz would offer her a lift. It'd be nice. Tomorrow was Saturday and they could laze around. Jane had nothing planned all day, deliberately in fact. Liz would spoil her as she always had done, making the coffee and getting the papers. Lately Jane had been feeling aggrieved by the overtly post-coital couples that lolloped into the newsagent at the weekend.

They started to think about paying.

'Come back with you, shall I?'

Liz put an arm round her. 'I don't think that'd be such a good idea, sweetheart.'

As they sorted out tips and change, Jane remembered the other two women. She'd been so intent on deciphering Liz that she'd forgotten to monitor them. Now they were ready to leave too, and as Legs pulled Tiny off the stool she whispered something in her ear.

'What? I can't hear?'

She repeated it louder. 'Our waitress looks like Robert De Niro.'

Jane craned round, and it was true: same colouring, same hair, and beauty spot.

Giggling, Legs and Tiny skittered off towards the

big glass doors, totally wrapped up in each other. By the time Jane and Liz bundled out through it a few seconds later, they had gone. It was drizzling and the street was almost empty, but a red car was parked across the road with someone inside it, reading. The car lights flashed as Liz ran over, and Jane followed, surprised. Rose leant across to open the passenger door.

'Hi, babe. I wanted to surprise you and take you home, but I thought it was unfair to gatecrash your reunion!'

She smiled at Jane, who smiled back, rather confused. How did she know I was here? I suppose Liz told her. How amazing.

Liz giggled. 'Hey, I'm getting drenched here.' She pecked Jane on the cheek and slid into the passenger seat. 'You've got your car, haven't you? Give us a ring sometime.' She shut the door and off they went.

Jane, watching the car jaunt out of sight, sank down on the greasy kerb. Give us a ring. Us? That meant they were a couple. Not possible. What had happened to Laurie, for Christ's sake? Give us a ring sometime. Sometime? That meant not tomorrow but in a while. It meant at a stage substantially in the future when we might conceivably feel like seeing you again. God. Nothing planned for tomorrow. Nothing planned all weekend. She'd been banking on . . . on being seduced by lonely old Liz. For old time's sake. How on earth had Liz got Rose? Were they living together? Hadn't

Liz noticed that she was drunk? Wasn't Liz worried about how she was going to get home?

Jane decided that she couldn't face the last tube, but equally she didn't have enough cash for a taxi. She started walking, and as she turned the first corner she passed a misted-up car. She knew without looking that the two indistinct figures snogging and groping inside were the women from the wine bar. Somehow she managed not to turn round and stare but carried on walking. Her boots were pinching badly now and the drizzle had turned into stinging rain.

Boys and Girls

CAREY'S GIRLS moved together in a tantalising
shoal; exotic birds, wind-up toys, they
chattered and sparkled as they shimmied
down their pavement catwalks. There were seven or
eight of them, and they worked in Carey's café
between more glamorous gigs as knitwear models and
car-show hostesses. Nathalie the dancer had eloquent
fluttery wrists and pepper-dark freckles spattered
across a golden face. Anya was savvy, black and
stunning, a boyish model with no hips or tits. Sam,
pocket-sized in fairy frocks, styled new bands and
Cleo was the creamy blonde singer erupting out of her
singlet and shorts. This iridescent core lit up Carey's
café and the rest orbited erratically round them: Ellie,
Lottie, and her younger sister Sair, who only helped
out if there was an outbreak of auditions or 'flu.

They had all attended the same dodgy performing
arts college and been inseparable wannabes ever
since: models wanting to act, dancers and backing
singers hoping to go solo. Anya was briefly on
billboards all over Crete advertising ice cream, and

Cleo once did a few stints in a helicopter reporting on tailbacks for a local radio station. She'd met the ratty little producer at a party and he'd fancied her; well, according to the other girls. As they sashayed through the tables, expertly juggling soup and baguettes, they would mouth at each other, 'You go for it, babe. You tell him.' Jobs and boyfriends disappointed in equal measure and were instantly spun or reconfigured. None of the girls were into girls, but Carey was still intrigued by the proprietorial way they touched one another, licking fingertips to smooth down eyebrows, adjust bra straps and even hoik up errant thongs. Radiantly provocative, they had no secrets from each other and knew that they were beautiful. They were unmarked by malice or the flavoured vodkas they downed in cheeky little shots. Carey's strutting dolly birds were sweet as coloured lollipops and innocently loyal. At least that's what he assumed until the electrifying Wednesday morning when his pleasantly uneventful life tripped over itself and stopped for good.

The girls hung out between shifts under the café in a dusty brick glory hole where Carey kept his spare sauces and paper napkins. They'd customised it with clip-on lights, plastic flowers and favoured icons ripped from the magazines that they restlessly consumed and then abandoned in drifts on the floor: Kate Moss, Isabella Rossellini in different coloured wigs, the young George Best, and Carey's favourite,

Sean Penn smoking in silhouette on a yacht. From time to time their advice was sought. 'Shall we check out that new cocktail place in town, Georgie boy?' or, 'Should I give him the elbow? How would you play it, Kate?' Sometimes the girls read as if they were one single figure with multicoloured hair and octopus limbs, interrupting, admonishing, reconsidering. Screams of derision would drown Cleo's claim that she was on the wagon or Sam's that she didn't do one-night stands. If Carey had to fetch something when one of them was changing, they weren't remotely bothered, didn't lower their voices or turn away, as they sensed, quite correctly, that he would never be interested in them physically. His flat above the café remained strictly out of bounds, however, and that's how it had to be for his peace of mind. Besides, he had never got to grips with the girls' own living arrangements – various flats in various places that replicated the harmony of their interchangeable shifts. Someone got serious with her boyfriend and moved out, and someone one else moved in or graduated from the couch to the smallest bedroom. Nathalie and Anya's place was just down the road, above the pizzeria on the green, and they used to nip back there sometimes in their breaks. Once Carey went to a party in that flat, but didn't stay long as eating and drinking with his employees made him uncomfortable.

Carey would let them swap shifts for a sudden audition but was unforgiving over lapses in hygiene, binning flyblown cakeage and berating the staff over unmopped tables. He did care for his girls, though, willingly misleading the tax man or proffering a shoulder for their emotional and professional disappointments to be cried out on. They found his detached perspective on their mishaps reassuring and he liked all of them very much. He had less in common with their boyfriends, good-looking musicians and actors, who were often Mediterranean or mixed race. There was one guy, though, Pierre, a graphic designer with whom he had always felt comfortable. Carey delighted in watching through the café window as this charming big-nosed boy finished his macho sans filtre. Greedily he would fill his lungs, exhale hard, and then, squinting against the smoke, grind out the dog-end with his heel. Pierre had never assumed that because Carey ran a café he couldn't engage with subjects other than stroppy customers or the weather. They chatted as Pierre paced and drummed, waiting for Anya to change and leave with him so that he could light up again. He seemed to understand why Carey had gone to such lengths to source the perfect shade for the woodwork and counter in the café. It was a soft greyish-blue gloss that didn't look that special in isolation but sang out against the creamy walls and golden floor. That colour restored Carey and always made him smile. He could enjoy it endlessly and drink it in and it never read to him as cold or dull. Nor did it try too hard, either, and yell, 'We are a jolly café here, and children love us,' in the way that orange or tomato red tended to.

Carey trusted his girls implicitly and, looking back, tormented by his sudden downfall, still reckoned he had had every reason to. Besides, in his own mind and by his own codes, he hadn't done anything wrong. The lawyers didn't seem to know whether he would get a custodial sentence or not, but Carey had seen enough bad television drama to be petrified about what would happen to him if he were unlucky enough to be incarcerated. The word nonce, a cross between dunce and nonentity, rattled around in his head like a hard little pellet of gravel that he couldn't expel. He had never categorised himself in that way before as he had never touched anyone. He just liked looking. Whatever happened and however it all played out, he knew that he would need to move somewhere else after the court case, somewhere where no one knew him. He quite fancied the seaside; Hastings, maybe, or Margate. Carey reckoned that he might just about dredge up the energy to open a new café, but he would certainly have to scour out his life and acquire some less dangerous interests. The police, the public humiliation, the exposure in court – he knew that he could not risk going through all of that a second time. Fifty-three was a funny old age to start over, though, even supposing that he did escape the horror of a prison sentence. His parents were dead and he had a sister up in Hull, but he was really only in

Christmas-card touch with her. Fleetingly, he wondered about telling her what had been going on but realised that he didn't know how to.

On the morning in question it had been warm and bright, although the sky had been overcast. Carey could still do a perfect photofit of that day – spring on the cusp of summer. He remembered nodding hello across the road to Tom, his GP, out with his toddler in a pushchair, before glancing back smugly at his property. His café had looked good in spite of the ugly 'For Sale' boards sprouting up all round it. That particular estate agency was ubiquitous, Carey noted tetchily, with its bulbous key logo and nasty lower-case font. Unusually for him, he had taken the morning off. There was no good reason, no meeting in town or pressing admin chores, but on Wednesdays the café tended to be quietish up until lunchtime. So, on a whim, he had decided to wander over to the Freud Museum and take in some temporary installations that had had good write-ups. He liked the atmosphere there and the almost palpable waves of history that seemed to billow down the stairs at him from the shabby plant-filled landing.

Leaving the museum, he had clocked two strapping builders tipping rubble into a skip. They were too old for his taste and stupidly lewd, he realised, when he lingered somewhat self-consciously to eavesdrop on them. Buoyed up by their muscular beauty none-theless, he returned feeling optimistic before sensing half a block away that something was amiss. No one was sitting at the tables outside his café. By then it was well after twelve and the pavement ones were usually the first to be nabbed. Looking across at the window, Carey realised that there was no one inside either, and that was unheard of. The 'Closed' sign hung lopsidedly across the café door, but he could see his own front door banging open.

Dodging through the traffic, Carey rushed inside only to stop dead in his hallway. How could there be voices upstairs when no one had ever had keys except him? Then there was another sound, instantly confirming his fate: police radio shash. As Carey processed this, feeling sick before he had even worked out why, two uniformed coppers appeared at the top of the stairs carrying his computers. Nathalie, her golden face a shocking putty colour, followed close behind with Anya clutching at her sleeve. Anya met Carey's eyes by mistake and immediately looked down at her feet, vividly shod in soft crimson slippers studded with flashing mirrors. He could still paint those shoes for you and get every detail right, as an idiot savant might. Why was that? It was like his near perfect recall of the weather and the birdsong on that morning. He wondered if certain details get blasted so hard on to your retina or eardrums with shock that they can never again be deleted?

The cops eased Carey into the back of a police car. That hand on the head thing was so absurdly familiar from television that he felt as though he were watching his own life happening to someone else. As the adrenalin coursed through him, he remembered thinking that at least the girls would sort out the café and lock up properly. Then, with a sick lurch, he caught up with himself. Jesus God, why was he imagining even for an instant that he could count on those Judas girls? Bastards! Somehow, someone, more than one person, even, he realised, as the police car accelerated, had got into his flat, his private, private place, rummaged about, turned on his computers, and instantly called the cops. Why in God's name had he gone out that morning? Why had he colluded in this fiasco? Perhaps the girls had been suspicious for months – was that possible? – and this had been the first chance they had had to investigate? Carey rarely left the premises when the café was open. His shrink had remarked more than once, in fact, on his apparently increasing reluctance to leave home base. What had made his girls suspicious? How had they got in and why hadn't they been on his side?

It was hard to say when exactly Carey's interest in pre-pubescent boys had kicked in. He had had a dull but bog-standard childhood in so far as he could recall it. Pasty, with girls' hips, he was never attractive, but had actually dated, even snogged, the odd girl, ones who were too hapless or lacklustre to attract anyone better. The boy thing had always been there, he supposed, but he hadn't ever been able to unearth it, or acknowledge it in any significant way. He had never known how to activate those yearnings with real people so had fallen back pretty happily on looking and dreaming. Carey had studied History of Art and had been good at it. 'The perfect queenie sensibility, darling,' he once heard one of his contemporaries sneer, thinking him out of earshot after a tutor had praised a paper Carey had given. It was certainly true that in that department heterosexual men were in the minority, outnumbered by earnest women and flamboyantly-shirted homosexuals. Carey liked it there, he felt good, fitted in – well, sort of – and even thought about trying to stay on to do some research, although in the end he didn't apply. It had seemed to him cowardly not to venture out into the world, for a time at least. Ironically, a lot of the things, images, whatever you want to call them, that got Carey going and turned him on, principally naked boys, were dotted around the world in museums and had actually come to his attention via his academic studies. He didn't like body hair, found the torrents and tufts threatening, craving instead the purity of smooth, flawless flesh. That was principally what drew him to images of pre-pubescent boys, as well as marble statues, which he sometimes dreamed of licking and caressing.

None of the girls had been near the café since that ghastly Wednesday. Did they think they might catch something? Did they feel embarrassed about destroying his life? That was yet another thing Carey would never know. There was total closure in one sense, but not in any of the ways that mattered to him. He possessed none of the detail leading up to the raid, and he missed his old life achingly, his girls and his boys and even old Mrs Manson, the most pernickety of his regular customers.

Pierre came back briefly to sort out the glory hole and collect some stuff. When he pitched up in the borrowed van, he was businesslike and non-committal; not cold, exactly, but certainly more distant than usual. No compliments. No clownish grins. He left behind a jaunty deckchair with a badly ripped seat, one dog-eared magazine and that was it.

The store room looked horribly bleak to Carey with every last vestige of girl festivity expunged. There were still the boxes of supplies, of course, dust gathering on the lids of the plastic cups and in the fat creases of the sugar packets, and Carey knew that he would have to go through them at some stage. Somehow, though, he couldn't quite imagine that moment ever arriving. He didn't have the heart to tackle any of it and accepted that the café would remain shut indefinitely.

For the umpteenth time, slumped in a reverie in the girls' glory hole, Carey went through precisely what he had lost. Day and night he had had his needs pretty much covered, pottering from his flat to the café and back again, and he and his life had interlocked comfortably. He had had only himself to care for and please, and that had suited him just fine. The waitresses had been his friends, as had those pretty and biddable boys in his flat, smiling and stretching and undressing each other. He'd given them nick-names, played imaginary games with them as he masturbated, always confident that they would never leave him until he dismissed them or ordered up replacements. He had been content.

Carey's disbelief and confusion, frozen since the police raid, abruptly dissolved into unstoppable waves of self-pity and he started to cry for the first time for years. Kicking out at the wall he stubbed his toe, swore half-heartedly and fumbled open a box of paper serviettes to wipe his nose on.

On a rare excursion to the bank, Carey bumped into Tom, his doctor, pushing his son in a buggy as usual and as friendly as ever. He invited him back to the café for a coffee but there was no fresh milk, the child quickly got bored and the modest initiative petered out awkwardly.

Then, stumbling through his otherwise featureless no-man's-land of an existence with the café closed, waiting for a court date and rarely going out, Carey belatedly remembered his friend Crispin. A nurse with sandy hair, a ferrety profile and a black sense of humour, he lived in Bristol. Carey had barely seen him in the last couple of years; since Crispin had been in a relationship, in fact. Crispin's partner Mack was a civil servant, nice enough if a bit dull, but the couple of times they had all met up, Carey had felt disheartened, realising that Crispin and Mack would clearly have been as happy, or happier even, on their own. Confident that his friend wouldn't judge him, though, Carey rang Crispin at the hospital; but he sounded fraught and didn't have time a for a chat. That was often the case when he was on a busy ward, and the court-case trauma wasn't something Carey could easily rush into. He did register with a slight shock, though, that he had had to track his friend down through the main switchboard as he hadn't known either the name of Crispin's current ward or its specialism. Things must have slipped a bit, as in the past Carey had always known what Crispin was up to – bones, kids or cancer – and taking that amount of interest had seemed a basic courtesy within their friendship. Carey reassured himself that once they had got through all the other more difficult stuff, he would certainly put that right.

Crispin didn't ring back, so Carey tried again and finally got him at home one evening. He sounded genuinely apologetic.

'I'm sorry I haven't got back to you yet, but Mack and I seem to get so little time together at the moment. You know how it is.'

'Yes,' Carey replied. 'Yes, of course.'

'Anyway, how have you been?'

Crispin finally provided his friend with an opening and Carey plunged in. His friend listened, said he was sorry, and that seemed to be that.

What had he expected, Carey wondered, carefully replacing the phone, its handset slithery with the sweat he had been pumping out during the call. What had he hoped for from the renewed contact? A visit from Crispin, maybe, or an invitation to stay, Mack notwithstanding? Certainly something more than 'Keep us posted, old chap'. That meant, in the politest possible way, that Crispin wasn't expecting to hear from Carey again until there was some news, to be posted about after the court case, perhaps. That was weeks away, and Carey had told him that. How did Crispin expect him to manage till then? Carey didn't have his girls, he'd never have his boys again and now it appeared that he didn't really even have his friend any more. There was grey desert all around him, and he had absolutely nothing to look forward to. He even lacked the energy to fantasise that he might not go to prison. He couldn't talk himself into little excursions as he hated leaving the flat and got increasingly paranoid that stupid thugs with school-age sons would attack him. He simply didn't know how to plough through the long, dragging hours. And then, a couple of days after the disappointing Crispin phone call, suddenly he did. He woke up with the beginnings of a wonderfully simple plan, and his depression lifted as he started to fine-tune the detail.

Carey was fastidious and cared about his surroundings. He had always kept the flat as spruce as the café, but decided nonetheless that a beltingly good spring-clean would be appropriate. With a purpose and a new direction to go in, he even felt faintly amused as he scrubbed, hoovered and polished. He also spent a lot of time drafting and redrafting the crucial email. Getting the tone breezily light was the key to the success of his initiative, as he did not want any of the recipients to suspect anything. He decided that whatever the sale of the flat, café and contents yielded would go to various charities, apart from a couple of his parents' things that his sister might like.

Carey was still seeing his shrink, which was weird for a number of reasons. Eighteen months earlier he had decided that he needed to talk to someone safe about his downloaded boys and the pleasure he got from them; perhaps he had had a premonition; perhaps he was simply extending his thrills under the guise of self-scrutiny. The woman who took him on never discussed her own life, but he had managed to glean the odd fact about her. He knew she had at least one child because he'd once seen a lad waiting in the reception area reading a comic. The boy hadn't even looked up at Carey, but, with his titian curls and small hands, he had such a strong look of his mother that Carey instantly knew who he was. Somehow along the way he had also discovered that her husband was a paediatrician at the Whittington. Then there was that bright winter day when Carey, to his amazement, had spotted her through his miniature telescope being kissed – being majorly groped, in fact – by another woman up on the heath. His shrink and her lover must have imagined that they were well camouflaged, and they were actually almost invisible, in amongst some shrubs on a deserted bit of the heath, but gay men chose it too, for just that reason, and Carey had found himself a hide-out to watch the cottaging from. It was when he was raking the horizon with his little black eyepiece that the reddish gold ringlets of his therapist had caught his eye. Their hands were all over each other and the other woman had a swinging bell of shiny dark hair. Carey had snuck away, knowing it would be good ammo at some stage.

A few weeks later, when he had felt that his therapist was needling him unnecessarily and over-stepping the mark with regard to his own interests, maliciously he had mentioned her girlfriend. She had jumped as though she'd been shot or scalded, a reaction he'd never seen before. A rash tumbled down her neck and a red glow shone high on her cheek-bones. She was wearing what looked like a man's shirt, button free, and held in place by a belt with a massive buckle. In her distress, the pink blotches rampaged down the milky freckled skin of her throat and into the V of her non-existent cleavage.

'That is not relevant,' she said. 'We're here to talk about you.'

But she was badly rattled. Carey knew she was. He thought maybe she'd end the sessions, but then reckoned she was too proud for that, couldn't bear to be bested by someone of his ilk. If it was a secret tryst, she had been pretty bloody cavalier. Carey had already admitted to her that he habitually watched men buggering each other on the heath, although he hadn't quite been able to bring himself to mention the telescope. He felt that using a telescope made him seem seedy and pervy, things he didn't wish to be, whereas owning up to watching men openly having sex in a way that he had never quite had the gumption to go for himself seemed almost acceptable. She was too cool to have made jokes about telescopes and cocks, but the connection was unavoidable; compact little tubes that you could extend and use to get yourself excited with. Even though the telescope rendered the action two-dimensional, there was still a kick induced by watching actual people actually come outside in the early evening, the air clammy with dew. No amount of wanking over images on a small screen could compete with that. It was less exciting, he noted, when it was people he had seen before, and the most gratifying combination, fairly inevitably, was a youngish blonde boy with an older man. Those were the red-letter days.

Carey stared at the bracelet made of faded blue string, frilly bottle tops and pebbles wrapped around his shrink's fine-gauge wrist and wondered about its history. What trendy London emporium had she bought it from? When finally he had told her about his waitresses' betrayal and the police invasion, she had twisted and untwisted her pretty auburn hair round her finger in the way she had when she was truly concentrating and said she was sorry.

'You don't deserve that,' she murmured finally.

Thinking about it afterwards, he thought, hmmmm, I don't deserve that, but I do deserve something. What, though? What do I deserve? Why is no one on my side? Even professionals that I pay a lot of money to to be non-judgmental are critical of me, find me deficient and believe that I should be punished.

Nearing the end of that session, he had asked her, 'Where did you get your charm bracelet from?' He had known that it was a personal question and therefore out of bounds, but had hoped that as he'd been having such a grim time lately she might just cut him some slack, and she did. She had smiled dreamily at it.

'Charm bracelet. What a charming description . . . Well . . . technically it's Cornish . . . my kids made it for me on holiday . . . It's . . .' She had gestured vaguely and then had shaken her head, the little window into her world outside his session had banged shut again. She had a life, thought Carey bitterly; kids, holidays, a lover even, whereas he had zip.

There was one basic email to send out, slightly customised for each individual so that the assorted recipients wouldn't register the faintest whiff of a round robin about it.

Dear —

You know that you've always been special to me, and because of what has happened I've decided to change my life entirely and, depending on the verdict, move abroad when I am able and live very simply. I've sold the shop and flat quite well and wanted to give you a modest sum. There are a couple of terms, with which my solicitor is familiar, and it's a condition of receiving the money that you come on this day at this time. If you feel anxious, you may certainly bring a friend or a partner, but not hoardes of people, please. I would ask you to acknowledge receipt of this notification with a yes or a no. If you'd rather not receive the money or have anything further to do with me, I will of course understand and have instructed my solicitor simply to divide the monies amongst the charities that I have already nominated. I assure you that no hard feeling will be harboured, whatever your decision . . . etc. etc.

They all said that they'd come and Carey wasn't remotely surprised. Most people are venal, and particularly so when they have been judgemental.

Carey continued to feel upbeat. He researched the different ways to achieve his goal, selected one of them, and the night before he'd bidden everyone to his flat, he went for a long walk on the heath. It was at its hazy, empty, gold, green, glorious best, and when he came home the café looked lovely as well – spotlessly clean, the petrol-blue counter thrumming in the dusk. He had picked out some nice bits and pieces at the deli for his supper and a decent bottle of wine. As he sat out on his tiny balcony at the back, buoyed up by the twinkling windows all around him, he felt properly at ease with himself and his surroundings for the first time since the ambush. It was mild and clear and he could see as far as the London Eye. Quietly toasting it, Carey imagined himself connected to its centre axle and sheltered by its rim, frilled tonight with scarlet lights.

Washing up meticulously, Carey dumped the rubbish outside, determined to leave everything in the kitchen fresh and pleasant. Then he had a long, hot bath before putting on new pyjamas. The door to the street was snibbed open but pushed firmly shut so when they all arrived the next morning they could easily get in. The wine had relaxed him and he felt light-headed but totally calm as he climbed into bed before realising that he'd forgotten something. What was missing? Ah yes. He hopped briskly back out of his big, high bed and flicked on the Mozart Requiem, set on repeat mode at a low volume. He did not want anyone complaining about the music before Crispin, with or without Mack, his sister, possibly her husband and of course the four waitress-girl betrayers arrived in the morning. There would be no money or solicitor waiting for them, but there would be a spectacle of sorts.

Carey picked up a neat little scalpel that he had bought from a local art shop and tied it firmly, blade outwards, to his bedside lamp. Plumping up the clean, fresh pillows, he wriggled hard back against the headboard to be sure of a good purchase, and pressed his wrists against the wafer-thin metal again and again. It was so sharp that he couldn't feel the cuts. Carey eased himself slowly back down the bed, watching the blood blotch across his creamy duvet cover. It looked like a Clyfford Still painting, and regret wisped gently across Carey's mind that he would never now visit Still's museum in Denver. He smiled. He wouldn't be subjected to the horrors of court or the terror of prison as a despised pervert, either, nor to any more betrayals or abandonment by his so-called buddies. So be it. This seemed to him a near perfect solution . . .

Whose Is It?

ABI LATHERED her shoulders and breasts briskly with a grapefruit and neroli bodywash, enjoying the different textures on top of each other: yellow slime globbing out of the nozzle on to her fingertips, wet goose-pimpled skin, and then fine-weave foam as hot water ripped into the gel. This particular potion verged on the bitter and was appropriate, she felt; serious, even. One did not want to go into a heavy-duty meeting with Parliamentary Counsel wafting synthetic extract of strawberry, or the penitential versions of soap her husband favoured. The gentle nimbus she would exude post-shower was perfectly gauged on the age and gender spectrum. It had been a Christmas present from Tim, her gay assistant, who favoured ebullient bowties and excelled in such judgements. He was one of the very few people whom she allowed to tease her.

Abi eased the misty bottle down inside a boot near the back of her wardrobe. She had to put a lot of effort into hiding expensive toiletries from her greedy teenage daughters, and they wouldn't suspect this boot as it had yet to be worn. A boot with verve, she had decided a few weeks earlier, snapping her credit card on to a distressed granite counter in Covent Garden. The reason it had not been paraded yet was again fear of her daughters, the elder one in particular. Her husband and both children thought she spent too much on clothes, and one of their fantasies was to hijack the tannoy at Harvey Nicks. 'Could Abigail Howard please stop spending money?'

Abi sighed. She had a long day unrolling ahead of her and she was gentling a controversial piece of legislation into being just now. Riffling through her hangers of suits, she hoped that the different textures might rally her. All the items were discreet and smart but possessed of just that extra funkiness in the cut of the skirt or the button detail. Her colleagues were drab little crows on the whole, but there was more natural fibre around these days, thank God, given the amount of time she was obliged to spend poured into packed lifts. Perhaps today was boot day after all. Daringly, Abi pulled one on over her dark tights with a satisfying new-leather phloomph and hopped about, twisting to inspect the effect in front of her bedroom mirror. Yes. Quite flattering. She had good legs and she'd been right to invest in the boots. What was the point of being high-achieving if you couldn't indulge yourself from time to time without feeling guilty? Wrenched as she was in any number of conflicting directions every day, surely a bit of balm was allowed.

It didn't do to admit that temperamentally stress really quite suited her. She actually got off on the adrenalin kick when she was required to notch up gears and negotiate yet another difficult work–home clash with sangfroid.

Abi thought of herself as unfailingly professional and that thrilled her, giving her a deep shine, she felt, like polished antique furniture. Paul didn't get much of a look-in these days, it was true, but that was kind of okay. Older than her, and a committed lawyer, he specialised in civil liberties, and that's what had drawn them together – they were both interested in changing things for the better. Abi itched her nose, considering her current, arguably repressive, bill. She wasn't afraid to get her hands dirty, but as a senior civil servant she was becoming considerably more embedded in the establishment these days than Paul would ever be, and perhaps more compromised. She did get a serious buzz, though, from the largely male pulse of Westminster and being right at the hub of the political wheel. She felt she was where she ought to be, was destined to be, and Paul sensed that and supported her in it. He had always been uncomplicatedly right-on, so they had far fewer emptying-the-bin run-ins than most of their peers. A dab of scent, or would it clash with the neroli? What was neroli anyway? Better not. Sometimes scent first thing could seem a bit pushy.

*

A couple of miles away over in Hackney, Val was also in the shower, having just ejaculated rather successfully into a condom into his girlfriend. Journalist and university lecturer respectively, they could afford to kick off their day in a more leisurely fashion than Abi.

'This loft,' he said with some satisfaction, 'is seriously funky. Rather like us, in fact.' Knotting the rubber, he bowled it with aplomb over the top of the orange and lime op art shower curtain. 'Goodbye, little bamberlinos. We don't want you today.'

'Don't, Valentine. That's mean. You'll hurt their tiny feelings.'

Val grabbed the loudly patterned towel that matched the shower curtain, and which his girl friend had earmarked earlier, and pirouetted gracelessly over to the work surface to make coffee. Sara emerged naked a few seconds later and skidded round their loft looking for the discarded condom. She found it, popped-balloon-ugly, draped over their DVD player, and squatted down in consternation.

'Where are you, you tiddly popetty things? Take no notice of that rough and insensitive brute. I want you very much. Yes, all of you, growing into an army of gorgeous sturdy toddlers, now, immediately, this minute.'

'Military imagery from you, Sara? Whatever next?'

Val started chucking small Variety packets of cereal at her back and scored a couple of good hits. She didn't turn round.

'Coco Pops are inappropriate for anyone over seven years old.'

'My hand slipped on the keyboard. On-line shopping can be quite tricky, you know. Oops, you wouldn't know, you've never tried it, have you?'

'Well, seeing as how you sit about at home all day, consume at least ninety per cent of the food and are absurdly picky about brands . . .'

By now Abi was in a Government car being driven fast towards Queen Anne's Gate for a briefing meeting. It seemed to her that they might as well just draft this bloody legislation themselves and be done with it. It would certainly save everyone a lot of time. Abi was beginning to regret having axed breakfast on grounds of her figure and to give herself a little more primping time. Tepid urn coffee might be on offer, though, given the hour, and stale croissants that people felt too inhibited to eat. Damn. Biting off the lid of a Day Glo highlighter, she sifted anxiously through her briefcase with her spare hand. Nope, it definitely wasn't there.

'Shit.'

The elderly driver caught her eye in his mirror as she started to babble apologies and executed a sprightly U-turn.

'We can still make it, love.'

Abi sprinted up the steps to her front door. She must have put it down somewhere without noticing. Paul was nowhere to be seen, but as she started to rummage through the assorted detritus on the hall table she could hear her two girls crashing down from the top of the house.

'Have you actually shagged him yet?'

That was Alice, the younger one. Abi froze.

'Kind of.'

And that was Bea, swinging into view with an exploding bag of school books. She was sporting her usual provocative combo of silver trainers, olive combats and a tight pink cardie that allowed her to reveal shedloads, as she might say, of annoyingly concave fake tan midriff.

'Kind of?' asked Abi, bemused. 'How on earth do you kind of make love to someone?'

'Mu-u-m.' Her exasperated daughter stretched the syllable. 'Please don't make us late.'

Bea focused hard and long on her mother's incontrovertibly new conker-brown faux crocodile boots. Then she raised her eyebrows meaningfully before spinning on her own designer heel, electing, presumably, to keep her powder semi-dry, for the moment, at least. Abi, having nervously rehearsed a number of put-downs, found her daughter's restraint disconcerting. Her children, she thought unhappily, were like wild colts. They tossed their hair, skittered away from her, stiff-legged with disgust, and galloped crazily off into the impenetrable murk of their teenage lives. Bea jerked her back into the instant.

'And if, by any chance, you're looking for a minutes-asylum-seekers-measures-meeting blah blah, Mum, it's over by the kettle, not, strangely, buried under weeks of junk mail which we could usefully junk!'

God, that girl was full of herself these days. Someone clearly was giving her one. No, Abi grimly corrected herself. Kind of giving her one. She retrieved her document as the front door slammed and the pretty retro blue and white striped storage jars in the kitchen rattled. They'd been a bad buy, thought Abi irritably. If anyone ever bothered to decant flour or cereal into them, they just went mouldy before anyone else remembered they were in there and used them.

Val and Sara were giggling along to the bus stop, with Val walking in the gutter to ease the disparity in their height. Sara, minute and opinionated, was a junior lecturer at Birkbeck. She'd done her Ph.D. on human rights and the media and was savage in her analysis of everyone's complicity, as she saw it, in a lot of the crap that passed as acceptable in contemporary Britain. Val was a journalist, definitely less informed but more user-friendly, which wasn't difficult. He'd been forced to leave Nigeria when it was thought that the rodents and scavengers in a special animal issue of the student magazine he had edited resembled the ruling party too closely.

Vigorously, Val hailed the approaching bus for his girlfriend, windmilling away with one foot still planted in the gutter.

'Honestly, Val, you do that as though we were in blizzard conditions, which we're not, and as though the driver were nearly blind, which he can't be as he's allowed to drive the bus.' She kissed him emphatically even so as the doors hissed open. 'Why don't you do something about this new asylum bill, Mr I care-deeply-about-my-fellow-persons-of-colour crusading journalist.'

'Because I don't think it's particularly significant. What new asylum bill?'

Sara jumped on the bus. 'You'd better find out, hadn't you? You know I'm out tonight?'

'So am I. I'm on at nine o' clock.' Val tapped his nose. 'I plan to be wittily authoritative and I imagine you'll find me irresistible!'

Running down the bus, Sara hopped up on to the empty back seat, whipped up her T-shirt and quickly flashed her pretty breasts out of the window at Val as the bus pulled away. An elderly woman at the bus stop turned to him in surprise.

'Who'd've thought,' she said in leaf-dry Aberdonian, 'that that wee girl would've had such big ones?'

He smiled, confused, blowing a whole host of kisses at Sara's tiny heart-shaped face, now disappearing out of sight. As she swivelled round and sat down, his floaty thistledown kisses transformed themselves into a cloud of milky white sperm in her mind, spinning and swimming through the air to envelop her.

*

Abi strode out briskly, talking on the doll-size pony-print phone which had been an inappropriate birthday present from her daughters, feeling a queasy glow each time her new boots clacked smartly down on the pavement. She'd be blissfully conscious of them all day, depressed when next week they'd got a bit scuffed, and by winter they'd probably have become old friends for hacking to death on Highbury Fields. She'd leapt out impatiently, getting on her mobile to Paul, when her driver had got snarled up in Parliament Square, feeling efficaciously time-and-motion. Job, footwear, family; with a bit of organisation she really could run it, do it, have it all.

'I know I'm away a fair bit, but surely one of us would have noticed if Bea'd got a boyfriend at the moment . . . No, I realise she's not underage, but she has got four major exams in a matter of weeks. Okay I'll try and get to the bottom of it this evening. That reminds me – prosciutto if you're near a deli at any stage? Gotta run, hon.'

Abi flicked off her phone and marched through Security into her meeting bang on time. It proved as tricky and debilitating as she'd feared, although she was gratified to discover that the croissants were fresh and unusually there was orange juice on offer. The rest of the day flashed by, with Tim struggling to keep on top of her diary and phone calls, juggling meetings and debriefing her on the move as she liaised with the Home Secretary's team before rejigging it all again when unexpectedly she had to stand in for her Permanent Secretary. Early evening found her hurtling down yet another corridor towards a waiting car as she berated an equally fatigued Tim.

'This is bloody short notice.'

Tim tried to soothe her. 'I know it is. They did have Jim, but his wife was involved in a nasty pile-up on the M4, and he's had to pull out.'

'Oh God, how awful! So that's where he is. Is Celia going to be okay?'

'We don't know. Look, you know your stuff, but just remember not to fiddle with your hair, it makes you look indecisive and don't worry, I won't forget to phone your husband.'

Paul got the message as he, in turn, arrived back knackered. To the police and Crown Prosecution's utter misery, he had got a couple of sadistic youths off on a technicality. Where was the fun in that? He put the prosciutto down on top of the junk mail and shouted up the stairs.

'Girls. Your mum's going to be on telly.'

Alice drifted into the sitting room, mock yawning.

'Allie have you seen Bea?'

Alice shrugged, turning away slightly too fast for Paul's peace of mind. He switched on the telly with the volume right down and rang his elder daughter's mobile.

'Bea, love, it's Dad. Give us a ring, would you?'

He kept trying at intervals of a few minutes and

eventually got an answer. Bea, in bed with a geeky youth with large red ears, was ratty with her father about his repeated calls.

'Give me a break, I'm at Jade's. You what? Doing our homework! No, of course I won't be late. What is this? Well you must be recording it, so I'll wait and watch it with Mum. Okay, see you, bye.'

Ears looked anxious, but Bea reassured him. 'S'okay, my dad just wanted to tell me my mum's on some dullsville programme or other.' Enthusiastically they resumed.

Sara was babysitting for her godmother, who had been her mum's best friend and whom Sara had lived with for a while after her mother had died. Her godmother had been invited out, the au pair had an evening class, and the kids were still so unhinged by their dad's recent departure that Sara's godmother was reluctant to leave them with anyone new. Sara liked the kids and was pleased to have been asked although it would have been more fun if Val had been able to come too as then they could have played at being a family. Her godmother eventually backed out of the door, babbling unnecessary instructions. She'd been out so little recently that she'd lost the knack, couldn't decide which earrings looked right or what coat to wear. She was going to the press screening of a television thriller made by an ex-colleague. Dinah had given the director her first break, and unusually the girl hadn't forgotten. It sounded fun; some of the cast would be attending, and Sara hoped that Dinah would buck herself up and get there in time. Encouraging her through the hall, Sara picked up a wet-suited Action Man sporting a tiara and a pink tutu rucked up over his tanks of air. 'Impressive lack of gender stereotyping,' she quipped, hanging him jauntily from a radiator, but Dinah only responded with a tight smile, more of a grimace.

Sara watched sadly from the front door as her large, bleak godmother awkwardly manoeuvred her bump behind the steering wheel. Unsurprisingly, since her husband had left, Dinah had lost all her sparkle. Her fairy lights were unplugged and she kept tripping ineptly over the trailing flex. That was how it seemed to Sara, anyway, on her third glass of wine, stomach empty since breakfast. Whoah. She put a saucepan of water on to boil for some pasta, confident that there were always industrial-sized bagfulls in the larder in that house. Then, just as she switched on the telly, keen not to miss Val, the toddler started yelling from upstairs. She'd lost her panda, she wanted a drink, a rug on the floor looked like a scary spider . . . All the usual try-ons.

Sara bounced up the stairs grinning. She admired the small girl's guts. Rabelaisian in her appetites, with freakishly large hands, she was always grabbing more stuff to cram into her wet, roaring mouth. She was the ogre's wife, running rings round her elder brother who was more of a bank manager type and took after his dad, the kind of wussy Oxbridge academic that Sara and her gang deplored. Briskly retrieving soft toys, moving rugs and refilling beakers, she finally felled the child with a friendly chop to the back of the knees, remembering suddenly that she had failed to press record. Damn. She'd been so preoccupied with Dinah's sorrow and then the little girl's refusal to settle . . . Oh God, the water for the pasta. She always forgot with toddlers how you needed to multitask like a mad person, but was determined nonetheless not to miss Val's programme in sorting out this little madam.

The programme was similar in format to *Question Time,* and Paul snuggled up with a resistant Alice on the sofa as Abi was introduced.

'I don't like that suit. It's way too young for her.'

'Give your mum a break. I think she looks great.'

Val, suave and amused, was laying into Abi on air over her position on asylum seekers, and Abi was responding with cool authority, reacting calmly to each difficult case study that Val lobbed at her. Skilfully defending the Home Office without getting in the least shouty, she only twiddled her hair once. She and Val both gave as good as they got, were clearly passionate about the difficult issues at stake, and the fluency and vehemence of their exchange made for riveting television.

They continued hammer and tongs in the reception area afterwards, high on adrenalin, quaffing wine at speed. But then, in response to a passing reference Val made to displaced children, Abi unexpectedly crumpled and turned away with a muffled apology, shoulders shaking. As she dragged an expensive charcoal sleeve impatiently across her eyes, Val propelled her into a little anteroom before anyone else had noticed what was happening. Sitting her down, he got some water, and then stood at a respectful distance while she composed herself.

'I'm very sorry. I don't quite know what happened,' she said, still breathing erratically. 'Refugee children and babies always seem to upset me.'

'Well, they should upset everyone. Don't you think?' replied Valentine gravely. 'But ideally a productive kind of upsetness is best. Sobbing into free wine isn't much good to them, is it?'

Abi looked away. 'You're quite right. But this . . . well, I hesitate to use it as an excuse . . . this is, well, more of a kind of hormone storm or something.'

Val raised his eyebrows. 'Oh yeah?'

'It sounds lame, I know, but I lost a baby recently. I've got two almost-grown-up daughters already, but, given my age, this felt like an unexpected last chance.'

'How pregnant were you?'

'Oh, barely at all. It would have played havoc with my career. I'm just getting now to the place that I've always dreamed of being, and I'm loving it, absolutely loving it, so from that point of view I suppose it did all turn out for the best. I thought I wasn't really affected and came straight back to work and so on, but when you mentioned those children, I don't know why, I just felt selfishly sad for myself, and that, well, I hadn't really mourned it or something. It came at me in a rush. I do apologise.'

Val nodded. 'Apparently women get a fertility surge just before, forgive me, they become menopausal. As you said, last chance, and your body is maybe thinking now or never again. Sorry, I'm being clumsy and probably making it worse for you.'

Abi smiled. 'No, not at all. I like talking about it. I haven't really had the chance to much, or maybe I haven't wanted to up till now. Have you got kids?'

'No. I've got hundreds of small nephews and nieces, but don't feel ready for any of my own just yet. My girlfriend's keen and getting keener by the day, so I imagine that I'll crack fairly soon. Who knows?'

A few days later, Tim, galloping through Abi's post, skated over a request for an interview from Val. 'He wasn't particularly helpful to you on that telly pro-gramme, was he, so that will be a polite no, then . . .' He scribbled a reminder to himself on the corner of the letter before lifting up the next item in his pile. 'Shame, really, as he's ferociously sexy and I'd be more than happy to make him a cup of tea. Moving on . . .'

'Actually,' interrupted Abi nervously, 'he wasn't really as difficult to deal with as he seemed. I quite liked him, in fact.'

'Must have been the way it was edited, then, eh?' Tim offered caustically.

Abi persisted. 'Well, I think I would like to try to help him out. When do you think we could fit him in?'

Tim flicked through the diary. 'We couldn't, frankly. Now, this dinner at the Guildhall . . .'

That afternoon, Val was noodling about at home, refining his shortcuts, in fact, when the phone chirruped. It was Abi, on her mobile, walking slowly over Westminster Bridge. Unusually for her she felt awkward. When he answered she stopped, distracted by a police launch bouncing underneath her and out of sight.

'Hi, is that Val? This is Abigail Howard. We met at . . .'

Val interrupted her, laughing. 'I do remember when and where we met. It was only a few days ago. Actually I was hoping to interview you at some stage.'

'Yes, I know. Thing is, my office doesn't exactly view you as a priority. We are very busy in the build-up to this new bill, but I felt I owed you one after . . . well, after—'

Val interrupted again, increasing her discomfiture. 'Honey, you don't owe me anything.'

Abi stared at the phone in amazement, stunned by his easy familiarity.

'I never kick women when they're down. Call me old-fashioned. It's the way I was brought up!' Val followed this with a roar of laughter. 'Joke!'

Abi was still speechless. Then she started to gabble slightly. 'Well, anyway, whatever. I would like to do an interview with you . . . When might suit you?'

On the designated morning, Abi was at home, awash in a sea of documents, having left a message for Tim that she'd be in around lunchtime. Pounding away manically on her laptop, she thought she heard the front door go. She had left it on the soggy Yale, a positive invitation to burglars, as their contents insurance document had made clear. There was a scuffling noise followed by an unfamiliar male voice.

'Are you sure there's no one here?'

Abi froze. Should she hide, shout or what?

'Why on earth would anyone be here? They've both got stupid jobs.'

That was definitely Bea, albeit a bit rougher-sounding than usual. Abi listened intently but couldn't hear anything else, so stomped into the hall to discover her daughter splayed out at the bottom of the stairs with her cardie up round her neck. A scrawny blonde lad with sticking out ears was sprawled next to her with his hand down the front of her combats. Abi raised an eyebrow, enjoying the rare spectacle of her daughter's discomfiture.

'Isn't that a bit uncomfortable?'

The bell went as the pair flew apart, struggling to zip up. Abi swept across the hall and opened the front door .

'Hello, Val, come in. This is my daughter Bea, and this is . . .'

Hastily the lad stuck his hand forward, nervously pumping Val's. 'Ben.'

'Bea, shouldn't you be at school?'

Abi showed Val into the sitting room and offered him some coffee. While she was making it, head cocked, trying to establish whether Bea really had left for school or just sneaked off upstairs, Val wandered back in, saw the brand of coffee she was using and said he wouldn't touch it.

'Fair trade is a pretty important principle for me. It's the least we can do, don't you think?'

Abi bit her lip, filled him a glass of water and picked up the tray to go next door. Val, meanwhile, was scanning her shelves.

'God. Aren't you even remotely concerned about what you're buying and from whom? It's not that difficult, you know, once you get into it.'

Embarrassed rage whooshed through Abi and she lifted the tray high above her head and smashed it down on the floor. Pulling three bags of coffee off the shelves she rammed them into the overfilled kitchen bin, which promptly tipped over, spewing its contents across the floor.

'Satisfied?'

Val looked at her unmoved. 'Well, as a symbolic gesture, it's a start, I suppose.'

'I'm incredibly busy and it was hard to fit you in. I

thought I was doing you a favour. I'm concerned about my daughter at the moment, and you stroll into my house and immediately start criticising me. However admirable your principles, I find you extremely rude.'

Val raised his hands in surrender and backed out of the door.

Shocked, Abi realised to her horror that she was close to tears. Sitting down, she took a few deep breaths, badly thrown by her uncharacteristic loss of control, and the ghastly pomposity that had bubbled up in her when she had felt threatened. Playing back the exchange as she unearthed a dustpan and brush she realised that she had sounded hideously like her own mother.

Halfway through tidying, slowed down by the sticky tea leaves that were clogging up the brush, her phone went, but she'd put it on message mode when Val had first arrived so she let it run its course before playing it back.

'Hi, this is Val. Look, you're quite right. My behaviour was unforgivable. Thing is . . . I really fancy a coffee and I'm walking past a place on Highbury Barn – fair trade, natch – if you felt up to trying again? If you're so cross that you've forgotten what I look like, I'm the handsome black guy sitting in the window.'

There was a long pause before he cut the connection. Abi took the phone away from her ear and stared at it, electrified. Then she giggled aloud to herself; she just couldn't help it. She giggled at his phenomenal cheek, but also with relief at getting the chance to substitute her intemperate rant for something a little more considered.

Outside the coffee shop she bumped into a fellow mum emerging with a mouthful of flapjack.

'Are you and Paul going to that school bash tomorrow evening?'

'No. What bash?'

'If you're away for the results, options if you don't get the grades. The girls had a letter about it.'

I'll kill Bea, thought Abi. She deliberately didn't tell us. Then she pointed out her date. 'What do we think?'

Her friend grinned back, impressed. 'Not at all bad for someone of our age!'

There were two large cappuccinos waiting in front of Val, and this time it all went smoothly. They chatted easily about everything, including the bill, before Abi, knowing that Val was freelance, remembered to ask him where he hoped to place the piece.

'I'll have Tim on my back for being foolish enough to talk to you in the first place. I'm a backroom person normally, you see. That telly thing was a bit of a one-off and I've never been interviewed like this before.'

Val admitted that he wasn't entirely sure yet where the piece would appear. Twinkling at her, he then revealed that although the bill she was involved with would, of course, be highly significant to large numbers of vulnerable individuals, he had just wanted to see her again.

'There, I've said it.' Val cowered. 'Better take cover in case you chuck coffee at me for the second time today!'

Abi was alternately niggled by Bea clearly having kept this school meeting from her, and charmed by the eccentric trajectory of the whole Val encounter. By late afternoon she had finally admitted to herself that charmed wasn't really an accurate description of what she was feeling. She was not only flattered, but almost achingly chuffed that a sexy young leftie had, well, liked her and wanted to see her again. She hadn't experienced these sensations for years – the skippy ankle feeling and happy, low humming deep down inside. Nothing could come of it, as she was married and he had a girlfriend, but what a boost, even so.

The next evening she and Paul arrived for Bea's school event at breathless running walks from opposite directions. Almost the first person that Abi spotted in the busy modern hall was Ben, sitting behind a table, wearing a name badge, talking to the mother who had tipped her off about the event. Abi grabbed Paul, hissing at him hysterically.

'I do not bloody believe it.' Paul was startled by her vehemence.

'What's the problem?'

'Bea's boyfriend is the problem. He's her bloody physics teacher!'

Over the next few days the battle raged. Paul was

tempted to turn a blind eye – 'She's only got a few weeks of actual school left, and it's not as though she's underage or anything' – but Abi was livid and determined to engage. Her strength of feeling on the matter took the whole household by surprise. She was unusually shouty, seeming to feel the inappropriateness physically, in her shoulders and neck, and shocked even herself with her inability to handle the scenario with any degree of calm. Having discovered from the headmaster that Ben had been engaged for some time to a nurse living in Wolverhampton, she passed the information on to Bea instantly with a frisson that was dangerously close to pleasure. The headmaster convinced Ben that his behaviour was inappropriate, and Bea was sent for her final physics lessons to a sister school, causing maximum time-tabling inconvenience all round. She was livid rather than upset, subjecting her mother to chilly indifference and the occasional cutting aside. Abi was unable to vent her anger at the way her daughter was treating her as she would have liked because of Bea's fast approaching exams.

The second reading of the Asylum Bill was also getting close, and Abi, feeling cross and miserable at her standing in her own household, rang up Val ostensibly to check on a couple of the quotes that she'd given him. He was pleased to hear from her, as droll and flirtatious as ever, but then, after that, seemed hard to get hold of. She didn't really have any further reason to talk to him, but his elusiveness read as odd and bothered her. Val didn't have the guts to tell her that when he'd been cooking dinner recently, trying to be elegantly fusion with some squid, Sara had kept distracting him at critical junctures so he'd asked her to check his emails. While doing that, she'd come across a draft of his article on the bill, read it and been incensed.

'Why are you being so soft on this government all of a sudden? Who is this piece for? The fucking Torygraph? Don't you care about what is going to happen to all of those people who will be sent home if this new legislation is passed? You, of all people . . .' Sara ranted on as Val, sighing, huffed paprika across his pristine work surface.

She was right, of course, and he toughened up the article, which came out a week later.

It caused minor mayhem for Abi professionally, not to mention endless I-told-you-so jibes from Tim. Abi was unrepentant if slightly rattled. Loftily, she told Tim that it would be craven to avoid discussing putative government policies with serious and informed journos on the grounds that they might criticise her. The issues were thorny and complex, with no easy solutions; she wasn't in this job to make friends; and so on and so forth. Quite clearly protesting too much, thought Tim accurately.

The pressure continued to mount, the politicians got jumpy and even Paul gently reminded Abi that asylum seekers were people, not a product or a percentage. She was impatient and dismissive, but then thought afterwards, how can I possibly see everybody that this will affect as separate individuals with faces and histories? That would, of course, be desirable, but it's just not possible. Added to which I am working to the Government and I shouldn't be getting any of this flack. She wanted to have the guts to own the situation, but equally was clear that she was a civil servant and not a politician. Val tried to ring Abi a couple of times after his article had come out, but lost his nerve before she answered.

Bea had now stopped talking to her mother entirely. She was in the thick of her exams and there was nothing Abi could do, except faff around in the mornings, wittering about the importance of a decent breakfast and saying lame good lucks to her daughter's unresponsive back. The weather was torturously clammy, and Abi's elegant linen separates got limp and grubby by lunchtime. She kept promising anyone still interested in listening that once her bill had had its second reading, they would spend some proper time together as a family. It would be the summer recess before long and then, surely, she thought, increasingly panicked, everything might stop unravelling.

On the day of Bea's last exam when the atmosphere at home had become unendurable, Abi decided she couldn't risk things continuing in this vein an instant longer. With a superhuman effort she got Tim on side, cleared her diary and went home early to make Bea a special celebration supper.

On arrival she found the house quiet. It was so rare for her to be there alone in the early afternoon that, for a while, she simply padded about in stockinged feet enjoying the sunlit rays of dust motes and Radio Three in the background before making a big 'Finished! Hooray!' banner on a fairly new sheet as she couldn't find any old ones. Stringing it up across the hall, she then blew up several balloons with great difficulty as she had forgotten how, and started cooking. After a while she rang Paul to check that he'd be home in good time, but his mobile was switched off. His colleagues hadn't seen him since lunchtime and thought that maybe he had had a couple of meetings out of town or something. It got later. In desperation Abi tried Bea's mobile, which instantly switched on to message.

Bea, Paul and Alice were sitting on the beach in their swimmers, surrounded by empty crisp packets and beer glasses, outside a pub near where Paul's mum lived. They were carefree and buoyant, giggling at ancient jokes. Paul glanced over at the phone as Bea switched it off.

'I'm sorry, Dad, I just don't want to speak to her. She'll only get at me.'

Paul immediately rang Abi on his mobile. 'Hi, darling. You're home early. I didn't expect you back for ages.'

'Where on earth are you all? I've been trying to get you for hours.'

'We're in Suffolk. I had the phone switched off while I was driving. It was such a gorgeous day we came up here on a whim. To have a swim and celebrate the end of Bea's exams, kind of thing. We'll be back tomorrow. Are you okay? You sound a bit quiet.'

Abi was slumped on the floor in the hall, tears pouring down her cheeks. The banner above her was slightly lop-sided, mocking her. She took a deep breath.

'Yup, I'm fine. Um, it's just . . . it's just, well, I suppose I wanted to try and spoil Bea as well, too. Try to . . . you know. Listen, just give them both lots of love, won't you, and have a great time up there. I'll see you tomorrow.'

She stood up shakily as one ankle had gone wonky, bent under her, and got the stepladder back out from under the stairs to take down the banner. She had unhooked one side when her mobile went.

'Hi, it's Val. Look, I'm really sorry if my article caused you any problems. I've been meaning to call to check, but I kept bottling it. Are you okay? Is this a bad time? Where are you?'

'On a stepladder.'

'Of course you are. Where else would you be on a Friday evening? Look, I know this is beyond cheeky, but I just wondered if there was any chance of seeing you, meeting up for a drink or something at some stage.'

Abi brightened slightly in spite of herself. 'Is now too short notice?'

'No, it's perfect. Why don't you come round here? That way we won't have to shout over pub noise. Sara's away at a conference. Are you sure you're all right?'

'I'm fine. It's just that I've cooked and . . . and there doesn't seem to be anyone to eat it.'

'Bring it round here, then, and we can have a picnic.'

Abi slung the food into the car, ripped off her work clothes and whirled around in her underwear. She pretended not to be paying too much attention to what she was selecting while feeling secretly confident about one pair of newish dark blue stretch button-up jeans – clean, thank God – that she knew that she looked good in. Paul had admired her in them recently. What on earth could she wear with them, though? Everything seemed too smart for this unexpected invitation.

In despair she went into Bea's room. Bea had nicked and lost quite enough of Abi's make-up recently for a lightning return raid to be legitimate. Obviously Abi didn't want to look too like a mum, but then again the dreaded mutton factor was even more of a spectre. Under a shambles of files, dirty mugs and muddled-up clean as well as dirty underwear, Abi came upon three, for heaven's sake, unopened packets of Muji vests. Perfect. It was so hot that a cream singlet and her swanky new boots with those dark jeans might just about be seen as acceptable for someone of her age. Shame about her upper arms, but she had seen worse. The Marlboro cowboy look or something like that?

Abi giggled. She wasn't herself any more. Just for this evening all her exhausting roles could be sloughed off and she would no longer behave like a wife, mother or senior civil servant. If her family could go away without even consulting her, then surely she was due her own little holiday from routine? Then, not believing that she was actually doing it, she sprinted back to the bathroom and put in her diaphragm. 'That wasn't me. It just got there by itself. Of course it won't come to that. I know it won't. Dismiss all possibilities from your mind.'

Val had arranged brightly coloured paper plates and napkins on the decking of his modest roof terrace. It really was to be a picnic. He was lighting candles in jars and spreading out a blanket as Abi arrived. They ate, chatted, ate some more, drank a bit and admired the view. Finally Abi stood up.

'This is the worst day and the nicest I've had for a very long time.' She stretched her arms above her head until her elbows cracked. 'Thank you so much for rescuing me, and now I'm off.'

Val escorted her to the big metal front door, leaned forward and kissed her quickly and lightly on the lips.

'I've been wanting to do that since we first met. The corners of your mouth just cry out to be kissed.'

Abi looked at him without replying. It had been coming all evening. Of course it had. She wanted confirmation that he really did fancy her, of course she did, but . . .

'Thank you for a lovely evening.'

Abi fled into the night. She felt as though miniature tops were spinning all over her skin.

Smiling, Val wandered over to his desk from where he could look down on her as she finally found her car door handle and collapsed into the driver's seat. She didn't seem to be driving off, so he rapped hard on the glass. When she looked up, confused, he gestured at her, grabbed a fat black pen, two sheets of paper, and wrote in huge capitals PLEASE DON'T GO YET!, holding them up at the window one after the other. Abi smiled, waved and drove off.

When she got home, she ducked ruefully under the half dismantled banner, made herself some tea, and spent quite a long time inspecting her kissable mouth from every conceivable angle in the magnifying side of Paul's round shaving mirror. She was sitting up in bed working when her mobile went. It was Val.

'Are you asleep yet?'

'No. No, I'm not. I discovered when I got home that I wasn't sleepy.'

'Nor was I, and there's a reason why I couldn't sleep. Quite a big one, as it goes.'

Abi giggled. Suddenly, in spite of the Bea traumas and in spite of the lateness of the hour, she felt euphoric.

'You don't have my sympathy. Go and have a cold shower.'

'I can't. I'm not at home.'

'Where on earth are you?'

'Outside your front door.'

Abi flew downstairs and let him in. Briefly, she felt awkward. 'I'm quite sweaty.'

Valentine's laughter filled the house. 'And you think that I'm not?'

He grabbed her, started kissing her and they had slow, leisurely sex for hours and hours on the hall floor for what seemed like the rest of the night. In her mind Abi had turned into a tiny precious doll. She was something or someone that had to be soothed and cosseted, explored and mended, very gently and very slowly. At one stage, Val jumped up, unhooked the lopsided banner and tenderly wrapped her in it.

'Are you okay, my darling?'

Abi snorted with laughter. 'Yes, thank you. More than fine, I'd say. It just occurred to me that inappropriate liaisons in this household now traditionally take place in the hall!'

'You could put the banner up again tomorrow.'

'Today. They'll be back in a few hours, I imagine.'

'All right. Today, then. Show Bea that you really do care.'

Sadly they agreed that any further contact would be impossible. It had been a glorious twelve hours, blissful, unexpected, and totally outside their normal workaday lives, but it had to be a discrete one-off. Everything must go back to normal, as Abi needed to repair her relationship with her family, concentrate on her career and so on. They both loved their partners and were committed to their existing relationships. He kissed her wrist.

'Shall I make us some coffee?'

'Mmmmm. Let's take it up to bed before you have to go.'

Hugging the whole night round herself for a little while longer, Abi grinned. Thank heavens Val would discover that her cupboards were now stuffed with squashy, reassuring, bright blue packets of Café Direct from Tesco. She'd bought lashings after the fair trade incident as a private salute to Val, and then lectured the rest of her family as though it were her own initiative.

Her reverie was punctured by mobile and home phones ringing simultaneously. Christ, had someone drowned in Suffolk, or what? Her mobile was still upstairs so she grabbed the hall phone as Val appeared in the kitchen doorway looking concerned. Even in her panic she was re-electrified by the sight of him – brown feet, blue jeans, brown torso and glowing blue coffee packet. He looked, not like an abstract painting, exactly, but . . .

She was needed at work urgently. Now.

Abi drove into town in a state of total consternation. God, she hoped that none of the early dog-walking neighbours had seen Val waving her off and promising to tidy up in case Paul and the girls came back before she could. Conduct unbecoming? She'd never been summoned urgently at this time before and her guilt immediately kicked in. How on earth did the Home Office already know that she'd slept with Val?

They didn't. Jim, her boss, the Permanent Secretary, had just resigned. His wife had died in the night as a result of her car accident and he had decided to look after his children full time. Abi was to act as Permanent Secretary until a new appointment was made, which would take time as it had to go to committee and so on. The timing could not have been worse with the friction around the asylum-seekers' bill, and the Government was concerned to minimise disruption. In addition they would be grateful if Abi refrained from appearing on television, doing interviews and courting publicity generally.

The dramatically increased workload didn't give Abi much of a chance to resolve her difficulties with Bea, and Paul, in his quiet, careful way, seemed to be siding more and more with his daughter. Abi's excitement at her extraordinary if temporary promotion was curdled by the cloud at home, and of course she missed Val hysterically and he her. They were desperate to meet, but tried not even to phone. In the end their resolve buckled, so avid were they for scraps of conversation or the odd grabbed encounter shoe-horned into any spare nook in Abi's day, although Tim was becoming increasingly suspicious. One afternoon they tried to meet for a few minutes on the upper level of the terrace outside the Festival Hall, but a colleague enthusiastically intercepted Abi and Val melted away.

Sara was becoming increasingly hurt by Val's sudden distance from her. He was courteous enough but their jokes, cuddles and fun – the guts, in fact, of their relationship – seemed to have disappeared overnight. What the hell was going on? He'd been weird, she finally realised, since she'd been away for that conference. Rather miserably, she started to check Val's email and phone for clues, and even resorted to counting his condoms, as they hadn't used any themselves for days. She found nothing to explain his behaviour, but decided that she'd had enough of this unsettling emotional oddness between them.

The next morning, when Val was in the shower by himself, she shouted goodbye to him, opened the heavy loft door, slammed it and grabbed a bottle of water and some fruit. Then she eased herself gingerly under their big double bed, only feeling secure when she was pressed into a dusty corner right up against the far wall. Val, gloriously unaware, pottered about, made fresh coffee, chatted interminably to a mate about Arsenal's prospects and finally got down to some work. Sara got more and more cramped and ratty. Apart from anything else she desperately needed a pee. She realised grimly that she hadn't thought this through very carefully. If he stayed in all day until the time that she normally came back from work, how could she possibly extricate herself? What if work rang, thinking she was at home? Given the current state of things between them, it was unlikely that Val would find her behaviour amusing. She couldn't reveal herself. She just couldn't. Then the phone rang and Val grabbed it. He was funny, tenderly suggestive, but nothing that he said confirmed categorically that he and whoever had rung were lovers.

It was Abi on the other end suggesting they bump into each other, just for twenty minutes, outside Tate Modern, as she had an early evening reception nearby. There were always lots of people around and it could appear coincidental, whatever.

Val agreed and left on foot with Sara following as closely as she dared. She lost him pretty quickly, though, and as she hadn't been able to hear where they were meeting, she had to sprint back to the flat and ring the last rung number on the phone on Val's desk. Abi, pacing in the Turbine Hall looked at the number that flashed up on her mobile.

'Get your skates on, buster. We've only got a few minutes.'

The phone instantly went dead and Abi was still

staring at it, baffled, when he tapped her on the shoulder a few seconds later.

'How did you just ring me from your flat?'

'I didn't.'

'What?'

Back at Val's desk, Sara tried again but the mobile was switched off and the answering service gave the number but no name.

When Val came home a bit later, he seemed edgy.

Sara tried the number again.

'Who are you ringing?'

Sara stared him down. 'A work colleague. You don't know her.'

Much later, when Val was crossly, crashily washing up, Sara tried the number again. Abi was kissing Paul hello, having finally got back from her reception and dinner in Southwark. Paul grimaced as her phone went.

'I'm sorry, darling, but I'd better take this. It's been switched off all evening.'

She flicked it open. 'Hello. Abigail Howard.'

The line immediately went dead again.

Abi saw that it was Val's number and shrugged. 'Dunno. They went, whoever they were. I'll turn it off now and we can go to bed.'

Sara was sitting at Val's desk, gobsmacked. She thought back to the evening of Val's television appearance. She couldn't remember much of it as she'd been dashing up and downstairs attending to

Dinah's children. Had she missed something? How frustrating. Why hadn't she been paying more attention? Now she had only the haziest recollection of what this woman even looked like. The more she tried to recall the detail of that debate, Val versus Abi, and any possible chemistry between them, the blurrier it all became. There'd only been photographs of the Home Secretary and a couple of junior ministers in the papers during the furore over the Immigration Bill.

When she and Val were in bed, turned resolutely away from each other, she tapped him on the shoulder.

'Val?'

'Mmm.'

'Can I ask you something?'

'S'pose so.'

'What's it like shagging a married civil servant?'

Val slammed on the light and totally denied having slept with Abi. When he realised that Sara had been checking his phone and snooping on him he became incandescent with anger. 'I'm a bloody journalist, remember? Abi is a mate, as it happens, and a fantastic contact.'

'A fantastic contact or fantastic for contact?' Sara enquired of him icily.

'Abigail Howard is much older than me, and, moreover, she is happily married. Now stop your jealous fantasies, stop stalking me, get off my case and perhaps we can get some sleep.'

86

Abi continued to be under immense pressure at work, and she and Val both felt pretty sorry for themselves. They were obsessed with each other but totally boxed in. They'd only slept with each other once, and only managed to meet up a handful of times in hopelessly constrained circumstances. Val was getting grief at home, Abi was terrified of being spotted too often with him, and there was no conceivable future, it seemed, for even friendship between them.

Sara, unconvinced by Val's angry denials, remained sure that something was going on between them. It demented her that the phone call that she had overheard had been inconclusive. She needed to know the truth, as the uncertainty was eating her up.

One morning, after yet another sleepless night, she saw Abi's name mentioned in an article about high-flying mothers who were successful professionals in various sectors. The fact of this particular name at that moment exploded in Sara's head, and, without allowing herself time to agonise, she rang a friend whose brother worked for a tabloid.

'Look, I just need to know. If there really is nothing happening, then there won't be a scandal will there? And if there is, it serves Val right, frankly, for lying to me and being quite so vile and self-righteous about my spying on him. For God's sake don't mention me, will you? Just say a reliable tip-off.'

Of course Sara couldn't control the press. Instantly

everything spiralled out of control, culminating on the day that the bill had its second reading, in published transcripts of phone calls book-ended with blurred photos of Val and Abi. Abi and her family were doorstepped relentlessly, Val and Sara's street was awash with hacks, and both the Government and the Civil Service took an extremely dim view of the shenanigans. The next day one paper led with the headline ABIGAIL'S TAIL under a grabbed and possibly doctored picture of Val walking behind Abi along the Embankment. She should have been anonymous and of little interest to the public, even as an acting Permanent Secretary, but in the dog days of the summer there was little other news. In addition she was rumoured, while still married, to have become involved with someone who was black, considerably younger than her and an ex-refugee himself while helping draft a draconian immigration bill. The media interest rippled on.

Somehow Abi held it all together, facing down criticism. Separately she and Val stuck to the line that, although they had become close, they hadn't slept together. What else could they do? It wasn't possible, because of the press, for them to compare tactics or even talk to each other any more.

Bea took the opportunity to move out, having first denounced her mother for hypocrisy and thorough-going flakiness. She got a job working in a restaurant, sleeping on the sofa of some dodgy druggy mates. Paul was devastated by the press hounding, the revelations about Abi's friendship with Val, which she hadn't shared with him, and the savage mud-slinging between his wife and daughter. Publicly he stood by Abi like a good spouse, although the papers weren't particularly interested in his reaction. The bill was carried with a narrow margin, and finally it was the summer recess.

One evening, when Alice was at a friend's and Paul was working late, the tight humid skin squeezing the city finally split open. Looking out at the novel downpour, Abi fretted about the deepening crevices in her family and in her hitherto impeccable career as a public servant, turning the worries over and over in her mind. Maybe, just maybe, she thought, she could fight like a tiger and ride it all out. Alice, Paul and even her mum were tolerating her but avoiding her as well, and it was a lonely feeling. Were they scared of her, sorry for her or critical of her? It was hard to tell. Perhaps with the rain everything would finally calm down a little.

Abi felt draggingly tired. She looked at her watch and reached, as a routine reflex, for a bottle of white wine from the fridge. Searching for the corkscrew, she realised, confused, that the pleasurable anticipation of the metallic fizz on her tongue and concomitant slight ache from the cold on her jaw was absent. The prospect of the viscous urine coloured-liquid in her mouth made her heave. Was she ill? No, she wasn't.

She knew with a sick stab of certainty that she was pregnant, and that the blue-line test tomorrow or the next day would be a formality. She hadn't had a period for weeks now, but hadn't really thought about it, attributing the absence to stress about Bea, or the Bill or the press. God knows there'd been enough pressure on her recently to eradicate her insides entirely.

Manically, Abi scrabbled back through her memory and her diary. How, when, what on earth? When she'd got pregnant before and then lost it, belatedly, she'd discovered that her diaphragm had perished, so she'd been very careful to check it regularly ever since. She'd slept once with Paul, fairly recently, she remembered; after that Southwark reception in fact. She'd hoped it was sort of a safe time of the month and hadn't wanted to lose the moment by getting up as she'd felt so guilty about Val and meeting him before the bash and all of that. Thank Christ she'd put in her diaphragm that evening before going round to Val's. That she did remember vividly. But something niggled away at her and chilly beads of sweat trickled down her armpits. Yes, she had put it in but then what? After she'd come back, she'd gone into the bathroom to admire her kissable mouth at length and brush her teeth and, yes, remove it. It wasn't that comfortable, so why would she leave it in for the night after she'd come back? She took it out, and then they'd made love. She'd forgotten that she'd taken it out as she'd put it in before going to see him. That was it. That was what had happened. She was pretty darn sure now. So this baby could be his or Paul's.

She thought back to the last conversation she had managed to have with Val. He had seemed pretty down about everything and had told her that Sara was moving out and was going to stay with her godmother. Although Sara presented as stroppy and together, Val was worried that underneath it all she wasn't that robust emotionally. She had never had a dad, her mum had died when she was still at school and so on and so on. Her godmother was pretty strung out too, her husband having dumped her while she was pregnant, and she was now close to giving birth. She might even have had the baby and how, in God's name, would Sara be negotiating all of that in her current emotional turmoil as Sara was desperate to have kids herself. Abi knew that she couldn't hobble Val at this stage; more to the point, she wouldn't want to. Anyway, this wasn't necessarily his baby.

Abi opened the fridge to replace the wine, looked ruefully at some brie, and then, squaring her shoulders briskly, depressed the switch of the kettle. Somehow she felt certain that this baby wouldn't fall out after a few weeks like the other one had, and if it did prove tenacious, under no circumstances would she consider an abortion. She could not, would not terminate this little scrap of a thing, whatever the consequences. God, what a mess. You thought you had one life and then, with a flick of the wrist, a flip of a coin, it appeared you had another – a completely different one at that. She couldn't stay with Paul now as it wouldn't seem right, living with him and the girls and waiting anxiously to see what colour this new tiddler would turn out to be. That would be unthinkable. No, she'd have to move out. And then when it – she – maybe even a son, think of that – was born, she'd be a damn good parent by herself. Better than she'd been to Bea and Alice, no doubt about it. Somehow she'd let the girls slip through her fingers. She knew she had, but this time round she would concentrate hard on avoiding the more obvious pitfalls.

The rain had stopped now, and, clutching the mug of tea to her chest for comfort, Abi stepped through the French windows and out into her garden. A soft blue plumbago bush sprawled over the path and she could just about read its tiny star shaped flowers twinkling out there in the dusk. Abi loved that colour and the charming baby-faced blooms. It made her feel that all was all right with the world, for a few seconds at a time, anyway. She had shoved it in last year during a passing surge of home-making and it had taken with a vengeance, even though no one had touched it since. Maybe she could take a cutting with her to whatever basement patio ghastliness she ended up in. Looking out into the wet-smelling night, she sipped her tea slowly and tried to engage with her future.

Television Sex

LUCY FIRST encountered him on television. She was heating up bottles in her kitchen and he was beating up villains in an underground car park. She rarely found actors attractive on account of their personalities, and even though he was unusually charismatic, she didn't give him another thought until eighteen months later when he pitched up at one of her read-throughs. The director had told her he'd been cast, and that it was a bit of a coup as he was just breaking into feature films, blah blah, but although she nodded enthusiastically, she was panicking about the lighting budget at the time and failed to make the connection.

The piece was yet another police drama squatting sadly in the shadow of its hipper, harder American counterparts. It was very male – whaddya expect from a cop show – with a token woman who was tough and able to handle herself, natch, but oh so easy on the eye and oh so much more lateral than her foul-mouthed hard-nut colleagues with their hard nuts, leather jackets and shades. There was also the requisite boss behind corrugated glass in a swivel chair who was crippled with a drink problem, a woman problem, what the hell, a whatever problem, and of course Lucy's underground car park man. He, she knew instantly, without even checking her cast list, would be that damn maverick cop who does drugs to preserve his cover, hits on older women, but by Christ he protects his junkie informer. Yes, sir! Wraithlike she'll melt off into liquid black night, beautifully lit in a ripped leather jacket with a bejewelled navel, scot-free and blessed.

A classic font for the end roller, mused Lucy, looking for somewhere to park; cream, perhaps, with a drop-shadow on dark blue. The agents will all be jockeying for front credits, clearly impossible with a cast this size, but they'll cave in in the end if they want the gig, they always do. There was still a bit of time. Whirring through her mental checklist as she swung into the gloomy church hall, Lucy reckoned that everything was more or less where it needed to be for this stage in the process. In the rehearsal room the baby runner was manically aligning ruled pads and sharpened pencils which no one was likely to use, but he was nervous, poor chap, and probably better off aimlessly moving things about. With a bit of luck he'd calm down once they started filming. Sometimes production problems solved themselves and sometimes they didn't, but the murmured request 'Could I have a word?' usually signified escalating dissent in the crew that did need to be addressed.

After the read-through the cast hung around bitching and sizing each other up.

Underground car park lit up, in spite of the endless no smoking signs, and wandered over to Lucy.

'What do you do for a living, then?'

She didn't reply as there were so many syllables in her job title that she knew it wouldn't roll off her tongue with the requisite insouciance.

'She's only the executive producer, mate. Know what I mean?'

The actor grinned down at her, unphased.

'Don't get out much, then, do you?' He spotted costume, exhaled and moved on. 'Christ, I don't mind what I look like, but, . . .'

There's always a 'but' thought Lucy, irked. "I don't care what I look like, but I want to look good." Or, "I know my character's supposed to be broke, but he would still have a bloody expensive watch and hair-cut . . ."' Actors, she coolly reminded herself; bogus by definition.

A few days later Lucy went out on set. They were filming in the so-called precinct and everything had a fifties cast to it: filing cabinets, desk lamps and clocks. It was supposed to be contemporary in so far as anything ever is, but the production designer had to make an impact somehow. What the hell. She stood behind a fake corner and watched maverick cop louche around between takes. His Irish accent was stronger when he wasn't actually filming and a good deal sexier. The make-up girl in a lime mesh vest seemed to think so too. She looked like the junkie informer and they were both called Lisa, although Lisa the actress's actual name was Wallis. It was all a bit confusing but undercover cop seemed to have got the hang of it. Tilted absurdly far back in the boss's swivel chair, he dominated the entire sound stage with his blowtorch blue eyes and lupine sexuality.

Even though it was uncomfortably warm with the space lamps belting down, Lucy was reluctant to remove her jacket and expose her upper arms. Itchy with sweat, she strode past the celluloid cityscape that was stretched behind the precinct windows. No urban view ever looked that luscious, but she adored its swagger and artifice nonetheless. She'd scooped the designer out of Light Entertainment where he'd been sinking in cheap comedies, and even the morose lighting cameraman was excited by the deep strong blues and dense blacks. 'Think supersaturated, think Edward Hopper,' Lucy had enthused, getting slightly carried away during a planning meeting. The older hands had rolled their eyes, long inured to what they deemed 'pretentious crap' spouted by young executives and invariably forgotten as the filming progressed. Obviously no one started out trying to make an expensive drama look dingy, but how could you keep everyone motivated if you were shooting across a long hot summer, there weren't enough filming days, and every corner was cut in advance?

The director was struggling with the moody, late-night, you-can't-hold-him-any-longer-without-evidence scene. It was supposed to be throbbing with unresolved sexual tension, the dreaded urst, as boss cop and corrupt cop both fancied the gamine, damaged prostitute. She, of course, was waiting nervously for maverick cop to show up, as he was the only one she trusted to protect her from her big bad pimp whom she knew would eventually be released for lack of evidence. Maverick would never arrive as he was being beaten up in an alley by imprisoned pimp's mates, that section to be filmed on location later, and so on. The director had been cavalier about rehearsals, and now couldn't get the blocking to work. She wasn't helped by the so-called tom being considerably taller than squat corrupt cop, which was entirely her own fault as she'd fought to cast her rangy actress mate over numerous adequate smaller alternatives.

After the sixth take, Lucy made a couple of suggestions. The director was hacked off but had to suppress her irritation because of Lucy's status. Belatedly it occurred to Lucy to blame the writer and script editor who were in the canteen doing rewrites so wouldn't kick up until later when someone would undoubtedly sneak on her, by which time Lucy would be back in the office and out of the firing line. The actors, disappointed that the director hadn't been comprehensively undermined after all, got bored and started making paper aeroplanes that dropped into shot, causing the neurotic PA, rather pleasingly, to burst into tears. Eventually the scene was deemed to have improved, and perhaps it was starting to gel, but everyone was getting so tense about possible overruns that it was hard to say. That tiresome director, Lucy thought crossly, would just have to modify some of her more elaborate tracking shots if they didn't make up the time. She had already had words about the shooting ratio. The camera department could be ugly, though, to female directors, and Lucy did not want to be seen to be siding with them. Really, you couldn't win, and that overweight camera assistant was as stroppy as hell.

Finally, as watery coffee was being distributed in grubby styrofoam cups, they moved on to the reverses. Location filming, with its heavy plant and starstruck passers-by, always seemed appealing from the vantage point of the office, but Lucy usually got restive after a couple of takes unless she was signing off on ambitious stunts. Being notionally responsible for it all, and having to fixed-grin into quips from men wearing sweaty tank tops in charge of the cars – sorry, unit vehicles – was never particularly rewarding of itself. 'Nice pair,' she would say, inspecting two expensive Winnebagos to show she wasn't tight-arsed or politically correct, but they rarely got the joke. As so-called management and not crucial to the minute-by-minute process, it was hard to embrace the erratic pace of a unit with special effects arsing about and make-up flirting in the lulls. Even though she lacked any specific expertise, the crew was expected to defer to Lucy in most areas, which made her paranoid about what she perceived as their perfectly judged insolence. She was terrified of tipping into the widening gap between the professional persona she was paid to project and her less authoritative real self.

When she'd had enough of the gossip and crap coffee and established that there were no serious technical difficulties or personality clashes about to threaten the ship, Lucy would ease her own exit by pleading urgent office meetings or a slew of budgetary problems. 'It helps,' Dinah, her world-weary boss, had once explained, 'if the crew thinks you're suffering as much as they are, albeit for different reasons. Visit the unit early on a Sunday morning when it's raining as that always goes down well and when you do leave, act sympathetic and slightly harried rather than overpaid, can't be arsed to sit about in the cold any longer.' Heading towards the fire exit and remembering this advice, Lucy waved at the line producer. 'It alarms me when you use the word alarm in a memo.' To his credit he played his part impeccably – 'Yes, well, I am alarmed by our escalating design costs' – timing his concern so that most of the art department filing past for their mid-morning bacon butties couldn't fail to hear.

As she left the set, Lucy pinched maverick cop's

arse and then, stunned by her own audacity, didn't look back to see how he'd reacted. Someone saw her do it, however, and fired off an official sexual harassment warning on the requisite form, which Lucy discovered in her in-tray a day later. Briefly she was alarmed, although it turned out to have been a joke. Ageing directors with bad perms and Cuban heels got done for groping ambitious researchers, after all, and this wasn't that different when you tried to defend it, although hopefully a little less squalid. She heard later on the grapevine that, his supercool persona notwithstanding, the actor had been startled by her initiative.

Back at base, bedandruffed youth were boring each other self-importantly in the lift and irritating Lucy even more than usual. She chafed at her desk, wishing for the first time ever that she'd stayed on location, and she kept hearing maverick cop's voice in the corridor. The following week he sent her a wobbly biro heart on a small, tight tangerine. She kept it on her desk as a paper weight until it grew mould and the director of the second block binned it in disgust. This director, Bruno, was good fun if a bit immature, lusting after stocky young grips unloading track and demanding endless wet-downs and close-ups of hub caps. An old mate of Lucy's, he was less gifted, admittedly, than the younger female director who had kicked off the series, but also lower maintenance. For all his wearisome campery and 'What a wet Friday, has anyone got any poppers?' he did care desperately about his 'product', as management consultants insisted on calling finished episodes these days, and Lucy liked him for that. She had to ban the poppers, though, when they started inducing cracking headaches in addition to their supposedly morale-enhancing function of making everyone on the crew squeak and giggle.

One evening on wrap, Bruno mentioned a party he was having the next day with his flatmate. 'It's quite short notice, I know, but would you like to come?' Lucy wasn't sure, and then panicked and pretended to her partner that it was a work thing. Recently their relationship had hit some kind of hitaus which they seemed powerless to negotiate their way through. She suspected he was slightly tangled up with one of his interns, but given that the pair of them had just bought their first flat and were besotted with their toddler, she wasn't losing sleep over it just yet. She knew that she loved him and that whatever was going on probably needed to play itself out. Given the way he was currently treating her, though, she didn't want her style cramped if the actor was at the party.

It was hot and crowded in the top-floor flat when Lucy arrived comfortably late. She couldn't get over to Bruno, but his flatmate Rosa was warmly welcoming if frenetically accessoried, with flashes of light bouncing between her ears, wrists and neck. Later on, maverick cop did tip up with some of his mates, already quite pissed. He winked at Lucy from across the room, but was permanently in demand, as effortlessly centrifugal as ever. His presence made her hopped-up and jittery, and she couldn't relax into the party as she would have liked. Determined not to embarrass herself by trying to monopolise him, she approached a costume assistant who was smoking in the outer circle around him. Sharp-featured and blonde, this girl made a desultory attempt to engage, but throughout their short exchange her heavily made-up eyes were darting round the room, signalling availability to all the men within range. One of those men, who worked in advertising, didn't seem to know many people and Lucy talked to him for quite a while. When, belatedly, it occurred to him to quiz her about what it was that she did, he did at least have the grace to apologise, for having bored on so about his own less exciting job.

Lucy started thinking that she should probably leave, as the scenario unfolding with regard to the actor was unsatisfactory. She realised that, foolishly, she had imagined either that he wouldn't show up, or that he would and they would have a good time together. It was already Saturday morning, and her son would be crashing about demanding her attention from dawn. She really did need to leave now if she was to avoid being knackered and ratty for the entire weekend. The actor, well ensconced, drinking and laughing, was still surrounded by a tight knot of his cronies, so Lucy couldn't even catch his eye to gesture goodbye. But then unexpectedly, he flicked his ash into a paper cup and started to dance. His tight, faded T-shirt , scuffed cowboy boots and inch of cigarette all coalesced perfectly.

Most of the party was aware of him now and he of them. The low lighting sparked off his belt buckle, his floppy dark hair did its thing impeccably and his eyes were the same colour as his ancient jeans. He looked airbrushed and elaborately styled, lacking only the tumbleweed and desert setting projected behind him. To Lucy's chagrin, Bruno spotted her unguarded look of adoration and did elaborate kisses in inverted commas with hip-wigglings. She mouthed a quick thanks at Rosa and left.

What on earth, she wondered, flapping girlishly through the drizzle at distant lit-up taxis, had she imagined might occur? That underground car park man would seek her out in front of everyone? Whisper sweet nothings in her ear? She had a partner and a young child. Yes, she was the executive producer of the show, so he'd take care to keep in with her, flirt with her even; but seriously fancy her when he had his pick of snake-hipped actresses? Hardly! As her cab swooped back past the house where the party had been, Lucy glimpsed the advertising guy she'd been talking to at the party. He had his arm round the tiresome sharp-featured blonde. The raindrops on the side window ran together as the cab cornered badly and Lucy couldn't see them any longer. She smiled ruefully, fairly sure they hadn't been together inside. Oh well, that was what parties were for.

Against the odds, all the precinct stuff on the sound stage was completed on schedule and the unit moved to Liverpool. The evening that Lucy went up there the actors were clowning around in the chalet-style bar of a Holiday Inn, and Bruno was flirting outrageously with the baby runner who'd been so nervous at the read-through. Lucy beckoned her director over.

'I think you should back off.' Bruno grinned and put his finger against her lips. He was so relaxed and touchy-feely with everyone it was unsettling.

'What makes you think I'm planning to jump on him? I'm giving him helpful advice about the industry.'

'Yeah, right.'

Attempting a lofty retreat, Lucy almost tripped over cuckolded heart of gold with a flapping mac cop who was flailing about drunkenly. The best actor of the bunch, he wasn't being stretched, his stories, the lighter B and C strands, only requiring him to fuck up and fall in the canal during a chase or hit on his promiscuous ex. In his opinion, a dishy drama-school peer in a rural medical hit was total and utter shite. Everyone intemperately yelled agreement and ordered more beer. Lucy, feeling tense and loosely aroused at the same time, couldn't push her face into the requisite shapes and emphatically did not want to imbibe any more cold and gassy liquid.

Looking round to check on Bruno, she saw that

amazingly he appeared to have taken her warning to heart and was holed up in a corner with his big-boned assistant, Rosemary. Unfailingly curmudgeonly and about to retire, she was notorious, and strode around barelegged whatever the conditions. This was her last show and Bruno was chatting to her, giggling and expostulating with every semblance of enjoyment, even though, after a hard week's shoot, schmoozing the younger actors and crew members would have been much more to his taste. Often gay men had better manners and were more compassionate than their straight counterparts, mused Lucy idly. Heterosexual male television directors, though, invariably self-regarding and desperate to make movies, had to be the slimiest species that the nasty swamp of television drama ever spawned. Going off to bed, Lucy wondered how pissed she actually was. Drink always made her vehement.

Sinking into a savagely hot bath, she exploited every last hotel potion as well as all the towels marching along the shiny towel-rail. If her son had been around she would happily have told him a story, with the different-sized towels being a family and the flannel their naughty little dog. Remembering, though, how real-life big daddy bath sheet was behaving at the moment, Lucy lost heart and climbed into bed. Fragrant to the point of dull, she thought irritably, squiggling about and fantasising. At three in the morning. she was still restlessly awake. Wrapping herself in a medium-sized towel, the au pair towel perhaps, in the story for her son, she wandered down the corridor. The actor's door was ajar and he was smoking a joint, fully dressed, watching telly with all the lights on.

'Hi. What you up to?' He didn't seem to get it. She lounged carefully on the bed.

'Couldn't sleep.' Then she stood up again, uncomfortable with the towel arrangement. 'Just thought maybe I could kiss you goodnight.'

He put down the joint and they started kissing. Then he put his hand down the front of her towel. 'Nice breasts.' That, she thought, laughing at herself, was a bit of a high point, and in her head she growled at him, 'Get your kecks off!' In reality though, suddenly assaulted by nerves, she stopped kissing him and offered squeakily to go back to her room.

'Yeah, or you could stay and kiss me some more.'

He grinned back at her through the smoke as Lucy, horribly conscious of the creases in her post-childbirth belly, fumbled for the light switches and failed to turn off the telly. Taking a final pull on his spliff, calmly he located the remote and extinguished both light and sound with an ironic flourish. Although it was suffocatingly dark, Lucy still had a strong sense of him and the sex, surprisingly, was sexy. She felt safe in the clean nest of sheets, the warm room encircled by the hotel, and Liverpool itself, all spreading away in rippling concentric circles, insulating her from her other life, her toddler and difficult partner miles away in a different zone. Fleetingly, she did wonder if you could get Aids from giving someone a blow job, but it didn't seem likely.

At five in the morning she decided that she ought to leave, and undercover laughed at her from under the covers.

'Now you've got what you came for you're off. Don't be so male! Stay and cuddle me for a while.'

She woke up later to the smell of toast, sticky with heightened sensations as sunshine poured through her curtains. She could hear Lisa, Wallis, whatever her name was, yabbering in the stairwell.

'He completely overslept. Costume had to go into his room and drag him out of bed. Literally.'

Thank God, Lucy thought. Thank Christ I wasn't still there. She smiled complacently, replaying as much of the night as she could remember while quickly showering, grabbing a banana and skipping off to watch the filming.

Outside it was clear and bright, and the crew and their plant were straggled across a grungy low-rise estate. Lucy felt great – slightly speedy from lack of sleep, but with a good haircut, thankfully, and stylish designer shades that Bruno had recommended a few weeks earlier. Blue-eyes, by contrast, was chalk white and kept forgetting his lines, but did somehow contrive to acknowledge her wryly, affectionately even, each time he wiped frame.

Bruno was capering about in a baseball cap that said Bad Hair Day. 'What's wrong with you, mate? Get it together can't you?' He shimmied over in Lucy's direction. 'Is he on something? Doesn't look like he slept at all.'

Fortunately before she could concoct a neutral and non-judgemental reply, Bruno was summoned by the gaffer with an urgent query about gels. Lucy turned round to track her actor, but to her disappointment she was seconds too late. Still whey-faced, he was being whirled off to the next location before she had had a chance to say goodbye or even exchange a complicit thumbs-up. She couldn't miss her London train as it would be too complicated domestically to change arrangements at this stage. How grim. Squinting after the departing car, she saw make-up flag down the driver and hop in next to him in the back. She imagined the actor settling his arm round those slim fake-tan shoulders and starting to crack jokes.

On screen during the edit, undercover was more persuasive than anyone had dared hope for. Lucy didn't see him in the flesh again though until the morning of the press launch. It was being held miles from anywhere in a condemned bingo hall, an offbeat idea of the new publicity girl's that seemed pointless to everyone else. Bright-eyed support staff swarmed round attentively, and even though Lucy was in charge she found that she didn't have a lot to do. When maverick strolled in late, as cool as you like, oozing charm in parchment linen shirtage and a dark, unstructured suit, nervously she kept flicking her hair back. He kissed her hello. 'Liverpool was great, wasn't it? Have you met my girlfriend?' He seemed completely unfazed, fooling around, spilling puff pastry on the faded fifties carpet and winking at female journos, which could be said to be helpful, Lucy supposed.

The critics loved the show but it clashed with a brasher, camper gangster saga on another channel, and no one watched it on transmission. The ratings were dismal, but the series did Bruno proud, catapulting him up a league. Six months later Lucy bumped into him on the tube with the young runner, who was clutching an enormous camellia. They had heard on the location grapevine that Rosemary was in intensive care with some sort of respiratory problem, and were on their way to visit her at a bleak-sounding hospital in the East End. Bless, thought Lucy absently, asking for the ward name and making a mental note to send Rosemary a card herself when she got home, while knowing that probably she couldn't quite be bothered.

That autumn, blue eyes was on the cover of the *Radio Times,* sprawled in a gutter, pink neon bouncing off his cheekbones, promoting a big-budget drama about the homeless. The publicity shot, Lucy thought acidly, was more than somewhat overproduced, given the subject matter, and would have been more appropriate as a beer ad. She cut it out, even so, carefully propping it up on her kitchen mantelpiece amongst the assorted detritus of dusty pasta pictures from nursery and smear test reminders.

'You should take a flame-thrower to that wall,' growled her child's father when, months later, he noticed the dog-eared cutting and ripped it in half. 'I don't want my son looking at that talentless lump of shit.'

Eventually Lucy's partner had admitted to having got tangled up with someone at work, and Lucy, not wanting to be perceived as a victim, had confessed to her own one-night adventure in Liverpool. Predictably, if absurdly, Lucy's partner had gone bananas, but a part of her felt reassured that he minded so much. Irrespective of what he'd been up to himself, she'd been unfaithful to him and, even though the encounter had been wildly exhilarating, she knew she couldn't ever risk anything like that again. There was too much at stake. Look at Dinah, her harried boss, single with three kids, poor cow, and struggling to hold it together at work. Lucy had found her sobbing her heart out in the loo recently, and she had claimed there was no good reason beyond utter exhaustion. Lucy would not let that happen to her. No way.

After the homeless thing maverick cop had become

a minor sensation, appearing in an art house film where he'd played some guy's lover. As if! It was the opposite, Lucy mused, of those monster grainy black and white billboards for designer water or 'eyewear', the ones where the perfect model on the beach with his arm round a French-looking girl and toddler absolutely has to be gay. His profile is implausibly flawless, his pecs absurd and his hair too styled for him ever to have been around the visceral shambles that is women and kids. After that, undercover went to America. Initially they liked him and he was in this and that, the sidekick in a successful caper picture and its less successful sequel. In the end though, it never really took off for him Stateside, so he came back, and married his long-suffering girlfriend. Lucy heard a rumour that he'd been caught shagging a transsexual waitress in a loo cubicle during his own stag party. She saw him occasionally playing eponymous hard-boiled and growling 'take care' to sad single-mum prostitutes in Fife, which usually meant that they'd be eviscerated by the killer after the next ad break.

The doctor's receptionist was still mad for blue eyes, though, and always bumped Lucy's son to the top of the queue on the strength of Lucy's past association with him. Lucy heard that he'd bought a house in Italy and put on some weight, just a bit. He was cheating on his wife again and possibly taking over from someone more famous in the West End. Lucy noticed that his lovely voice was becoming ever more familiar, caressing her through telly ads at first, but then, depressingly, one day when she was pregnant again and driving into work with her partner, providing the voiceover for an office supplies ad.

It was a grey day and Lucy was waiting for a knot of roadworks traffic to untangle and tapping the steering wheel as the previous ad segued into a cheap sting she hadn't heard before intermingled with photocopying sound effects and ringing phones. That was followed by a rhyming list of office stationery products, a sung phone number and maverick cop drawling lazily, 'You order we deliver.' Amused in spite of herself, Lucy shook her head. She had ordered – well kind of – and he had emphatically delivered. In her current workaday existence she still treasured that memory and occasionally still exhumed it to pep her up when she felt dowdy or sad.

Reaching across to switch to a funkier radio channel, there was a sudden surge and Lucy nearly knocked over the makeshift traffic lights as she accelerated forward. She looked anxiously at her partner's profile, but he was fiddling with the port on his laptop and clearly absent. Pulling into a side road and stopping to drop him off, Lucy decided that her ruddy, forthright little son would not be allowed to act. It would be just too humiliating being in a major American movie one minute and reduced to advertising office supplies the next. As her partner packed away his laptop, she noticed that he was getting a slight paunch, in sync, almost, with her pregnancy bulge. He pecked her goodbye without really noticing, and then wandered off to the tube entrance, failing to wave.

Watching him disappear down the black mouth, Lucy wondered if she'd have time to grab a second breakfast at work before a difficult meeting. There were problems with a key love scene in a new hospital drama, the writer's agent was threatening to involve the press and it might all ramify rather tiresomely if Lucy didn't pay attention. The baby rippled against the seat belt, and she twinkled inside at the thought of it, the imminent prospect of paid leave and Dinah having to field fictional hospital traumas while she was part of the real thing. If this was what getting older and settling down felt like, then Lucy reckoned that she could probably handle it.

Poison

DINAH WAS miles away, wondering what kind of sex between a paramedic and his male nurse lover in the back of an ambulance could conceivably be deemed acceptable before the nine o' clock watershed. Making judicious edits in her head and deaf to the phone ringing downstairs, she failed to focus on her daughter who was draping a grubby flannel over her knee. 'Sore knee. Make it better.' Catching on with a jolt, Dinah cautiously peeled it back to reveal the faint crimson cross-hatching of an ancient graze. 'Oof, that does look nasty.' Delighted, the baby clapped her hands, even though Dinah's attention had immediately switched back to wondering when the problem episode was due to transmit, and why the writer was being so combative.

'Mum, phone. It's something Brady and we're starving.'

Why on earth would he be contacting her now? Wet tiles spun and she lurched for comfort towards the foamy, preoccupied baby, who batted her away.

'Mum, what shall I tell him? Are you coming down and can we have pizza?'

The phone lay on its side on the work surface, a black monster poised to scald or bite her.

'Hello?' Dinah's usually confident voice sounded pathetic, a weak, trailing thread emerging from someone else's mouth. She motioned her son upstairs to watch the bath-bound baby.

'Hi, Dinah, I know this is a bit out of the blue.'

A bit? In all that time his voice hadn't changed a jot. The timbre of it tugged everything back up to the surface, stuff that she'd determinedly buried under other better memories. Her past was suddenly arc-lit by his voice. It all flooded back immediately: the colour of the tractor, the clods of dry mud, pin-sharp under a metallic sky, and the precise gauge of the weave of Sam's shirt.

'Are you okay? Are you still there?'

His voice was oddly light and cautious, given his barrel-chested build, and she'd forgotten that distinctive weak r. Dinah wasn't seeing the faces of the men now, only segments in close-up: fists, cocks, the corner of the cow shed, the ugly anus end of the gun and rough heels in dirty plastic sandals. She was lying flat on her back in a puddle with three strangers queuing up to take turns in her. The details, laboriously gauzed over with time, still had the power to smack her in the face and make her retch.

Had she seen Sam Brady again after India? She

genuinely couldn't remember. Just once, maybe, before they had set off for university to prove to each other that everything was back to normal. Yes, that was probably right. Dinah couldn't recall the actual encounter but could so easily picture it, fractured and woefully constrained, with her mother hovering in the background trying not to embarrass her. 'Hope your course goes well . . . See you soon.' Both of them would have known categorically that they would never reconnect, and of course they hadn't and that had been fine and that's how it had stayed all this time. Occasionally those horrific events still flickered across her mind, but that was a far cry from actually talking to Sam on the phone or arranging to meet up with him.

Absurdly churned up by the unexpected contact, Dinah emailed her best friend the next morning.

We weren't lovers, even, but what we went through was more intimate, I suppose – unhinged by the thought of him – ridiculously busy at work – can't concentrate.

She shook her head to blur the turmoil erupting in her mind. The doctors and nurses in her hospital drama were morphing into plastic figures in a pornographic board game and repeatedly forcing themselves on their bedridden patients in time to a hectic cartoon soundtrack.

Sam's phone call had smashed into what was already proving a difficult week for Dinah. The mice were really starting to get a hold now; her son had even found one scampering about in his sock drawer up on the top floor. And unasked, a local estate agent had nailed up a For Sale sign on the outside of the house. In her current state of unsettlement, Dinah started to wonder if she'd decided to sell the house without noticing, until a neighbour reassured her that it was some scam or other to make that particular company look active in the area. That's why they kept vaguely promising to deal with it but not actually doing anything. No, Dinah thought, she bloody well would not pull it down herself, even though the nasty purple key logo was looming over her baby's cot and unhinging her at night. The sign was huge, high up, and what would she do with that shiny chunk of wood once she got it down, anyway? It might lie out in the street for days, with protruding nails for old ladies to skin their shins on. No, no, no. It was the estate agents' property and they could bloody well deal with it. Bastards.

'Mum, are you okay?'

'Yes, why wouldn't I be?'

'You were sitting there staring at nothing and frowning. You looked like you wanted to kill someone.'

Reluctantly, Dinah started putting down little red foil dishes of poison at night to destroy the mice as they'd gone nowhere near the so-called humane traps. I must be more effective as a parent, she thought anxiously; rampaging rodents, invasive estate agents and failing to cut it at work, it just won't do.

As the dinner with Sam pulsed closer, *it's not a date,*

it's not a date thrummed maddeningly in her ears. We were never lovers because, well, because we didn't fancy each other, and now he's a married GP with two daughters.

She rang the Alan Sandler Estate Agency for the zillionth time and let rip. This time, at least, she got a nice-sounding woman who actually volunteered her name, Lindy.

'Look, I can see this is upsetting for you. Leave it with me and I promise I'll get back to you.'

The undate evening with Sam was almost upon her. *Cancel,* her best friend had counselled, eventually returning the email. *If you're not ready, there's really no obligation for you to seek closure on all of that stuff.* Although she couldn't bring herself to book anywhere or dress up, Dinah knew that she wouldn't cancel. There was a frisson about the disruption to her usual routine that she welcomed, while genuinely hoping that Sam himself might panic and postpone. He was coming on straight after his evening surgery, and, nervously, Dinah hid herself down in the kitchen, noodling about. She'd fed and bedded the baby rather efficiently and was now snapping repeatedly at her other two for no reason.

The au pair let Sam in before shyly disappearing back upstairs. Dinah's children stared at him, and sensibly he neither ignored them nor gushed until her daughter, belatedly feeling upstaged, whacked his knees with a grubby doll.

'What's she called, then?' he enquired of her, smiling.

'Mine.'

Sam raised his eyebrows, amused, as the little girl turned her back on them and stumped off upstairs.

A friend of his had recommended a restaurant within walking distance which Dinah had never been to. It was fine, nice, in fact, funky, with good food, and very busy. They didn't touch on India. The nearest they got was discussing her then-boyfriend's current lifestyle in New York. Always damaged, in the interim he'd become seriously misanthropic. Dinah asked Sam about his sister. His older sister and hers had been friends, and that was perhaps how they'd met, another detail she could no longer recall.

'It's a bit complicated. Bella's married with kids and has been having an affair for about a year. She's a banker, high-achieving and always got everything that she wanted – the husband, the house in Highgate, the three kids. It all came very easily to her, and now she doesn't know what to do. Amazingly her husband thinks it's quite funny.'

'What's the problem then?' Discreetly, Dinah tried to dislodge a shred of langoustine sinew that had rammed itself into her gum.

'The problem is that Ally, her lover, can't cope with the stress and wants to break it off.'

'Ali?' Dinah asked. 'Scottish or Indian?'

'Well, she could be from Scotland, I suppose. I

don't know where she comes from, actually, as I only met her the once.'

'God, a girl? I mean, a woman?' Dinah, remembering Bella's sleek, dark bob and bright lipstick, was stunned and didn't have the energy to be pc cool about it. You never had to pretend with Sam anyway; that was one of the many points of him.

'Yup,' said Sam, blowing up into his fringe. 'A woman.'

'What is she like? This woman?'

'Well,' said Sam, 'not instantly phwoar if you're a bloke, if you know what I mean, but quite, er . . . intriguing, all the same. Elfin, is how you'd describe her, I suppose: loads of curly hair, freckled, slim. Bella probably squashes her.'

Dinah tried to look cross. 'I don't think we need to go there.'

'No, you're right. Although Bella's husband wouldn't agree with you about that.'

'All men except you are perverts.'

'Yeah, and I'm a doctor.'

'So where's your wife and why didn't you bring her?'

'She moved back to France with the kids. She's a cardiologist and it was hard for her here.'

Fair-minded to the last, thought Dinah. That's my Sam. Why don't I bloody well fancy him?

'I go over to visit the kids most weekends in the winter, and a bit less in the summer.' Dinah didn't care to probe, although later in the evening Sam, in passing, said sadly that his kind of marriage wasn't very good for the soul.

Dinah found herself reflecting swimmily on the different varieties of pain within relationships. After all, she had had a physical relationship, albeit only for a few hours, with the three men who had beaten her up and raped her in rotation through that night all those years ago. She hadn't known them before that evening, and she would certainly never see them again. Whenever she had told the story since, usually in a studiedly throwaway way, as there seemed no other way open to her that wasn't either bogus or vainglorious, her audience were invariably electrified and concerned for her, and she felt that somehow she'd tricked them. The story of her long-term lover, however, shipping out when she was pregnant with their third child to marry someone younger with her own competing child, bored everyone senseless within seconds. How absurd perceptions were. The second pain had been on a different plane and in a different league entirely from the first. It still twisted around in her entrails, smiting her unexpectedly, and she knew that it would go on tormenting her for years and years. The smash-up had been vilely hard and she feared that she would never entirely make peace with herself over it. Fairly inevitably, her ex's new relationship was now faltering and flickering out, but that only seemed to make Dinah hate her ex-partner's new wife even more. Smash up my family, marry the father of my children and then lose interest in him once everything's too fucked up to be reassembled.

'Penny for them?'

Sam scribbled lazily in the air for the bill, and Dinah shook her head as she had too many thoughts to voice. She often felt that these days, even when she wasn't drunk. Her head was full of notions squiggling about like tadpoles, trying to escape through too small a mouth, by way of speech. On the few occasions Dinah had had cocaine, she'd felt as though she could count all the thoughts lining up in her head in an orderly fashion as they waited to exit. 'I've got eleven things to say.' Her listeners fell about, of course. 'No, listen . . .' But she never got beyond three and a half at the absolute outside.

In the middle of these ricocheting thoughts about thoughts, her baby's rounded knee, draped with the flannel, erupted unbidden into her mind. There was something bothering her, right on the edge of her consciousness, something she wasn't quite getting right. Perhaps she was finally losing it. Dinah tilted her head to see if it made the knee jiggle about amongst the Captain Matey bubbles, but it disappeared again. Sam, holding up the almost empty wine bottle, looked over at her quizzically. For a second she couldn't work out if he was offering her more or explaining why she was muddled.

'No thanks,' she said shakily, 'I think I've had enough.'

They walked back amicably enough, and just as she was inviting Sam in, Dinah noticed that the For Sale board had finally disappeared. Alleluia. Go Lindy. Its absence registered with Dinah as a little click of satisfaction in her head – one door shut, and therefore one less opening for her marbles to roll out of. No longer for sale she thought, smirking, even though I have as yet to be bought!

Her son, who never settled properly until she was back, came padding down to check on them.

'Girls okay?'

He seemed a bit tongue-tied by Sam and his bulk, but then brightened.

'Yeah, Mum, but you'll never guess what? Kitty learned to climb out of her cot. Isn't that cool? I played with her for a bit and then I put her back.'

Something somewhere in the recesses of Dinah's now unreliably tired mind flared up like a match.

The mice poison.

Shit.

She sprinted upstairs. Shit, shit, shit. She'd put the saucers down once the baby was safely in her cot, thinking she couldn't possibly reach the poison or be exposed to it. Dinah stared at the saucers, willing them to be undisturbed. Sam and her son came into the room as Dinah squatted down to stare and stare at the little foil dishes, hoping they'd give off some sign. She felt dizzy with anxiety. The baby loved sweets, and if she'd noticed the tiny, brightly coloured cubes they would undoubtedly have appealed to her. If, if, if . . .

'Did you hear her get out of her cot? I mean, do you think she would have had time to . . .'

'Dunno, Mum.'

'Well, didn't you hear her at all?'

'Not until she shouted from the stairs. I was watching a video.'

'Where was Jutta, for heaven's sake?'

'In the bath. Mum, don't blame her. It was my fault it was on so loud.'

Sam came back, having washed his hands, and went over to look at the baby.

'I'm sure she's fine. No sign of that blue colour round her mouth.'

Dinah's heart was still thumping. 'What would it do to her?'

'Get the packet and I'll have a look.'

Carefully, Sam read the box. 'Yes, it does still have warfarin in it. That thins the blood, so she'd bleed.'

'How? Where?' Dinah started to cry.

Sam swung even further into to professional mode.

'Tell you what. I've got some very precise scales in the car. We'll weigh what's left. It won't be conclusive, as the mice may have taken some while we were out, but it seems unlikely with the racket the video was making. If these saucers weigh the same as the unopened sachets, you can relax. I'll check her very carefully, but I'm sure she's fine.'

He went out to the car and Dinah scooped up the

foil dishes and put all the unopened poisons out of sight on top of her wardrobe.

Sam's phone rang while he was weighing sachets. His sister had left home. What an evening of alarms.

'I'll come over when I can,' Sam reassured his brother-in-law. 'This is more important.'

But then he was gone, decently, kindly, off into the night. He told Dinah precisely what to look for and what to do if she was worried about the baby. He needed to drop in on his brother-in-law and the kids, try and talk to his sister, and then he had the equivalent of Ofsted looming at his surgery with scads of paperwork still to do. He smiled wearily. 'It's okay. I'm used to it'.

Would Dinah see him again? Hard to say. It wasn't as though they'd been ripping each other's clothes off or even playing footsie under the table. Still, the whole India thing, without being aired, had somehow been revisited, at least, and even though Dinah often felt wobbly and vulnerable, she was still more or less in the saddle with her kids, unlike his sister. Could Bella seriously have abandoned her brood for alluring Ally? How long would that last? Yawning, Dinah decided that maybe she wasn't wholly ineffective after all. With any luck her baby hadn't ingested any poison, the house definitely wasn't for sale, and if sometimes the surfeit of detail in her head threatened to slop over into incoherence, that was hardly the end of the world.

It was now well past midnight, but Dinah's mind

was still racing. Perhaps some peppermint tea would help.

She turned on the kettle, slumping at the kitchen table while it boiled, registering lopsidedness as one elbow was half on an exercise book. Shoving it out of range, she noticed a practice maths paper protruding from it and idly flicked to the end where red biro shouted 'D. Poor.' at her. Christ! When had he got that? Hastily Dinah reviewed any relevant exchanges she might have had with her son recently, but could only remember repeated requests to him to look after the baby. The baby. God. No, Sam had been adamant that there was nothing to worry about. On her way up with the tea she'd check her again, make sure Kitty wasn't, what, bleeding from her ears or her nose?

Dinah heaved herself to her feet, still reviewing the evening. She must remember to ask her son about his maths and maybe hire some kind of pest-control operative to eliminate the mice. She'd had enough of DIY traps and poison. Where had the business directory got to? She was sure she'd noticed it wedged somewhere unlikely earlier, but decided she was too knackered to pursue it now. Maybe she'd have time tomorrow after all of those pointless department appraisals. Should she ring nice Lindy to thank her for getting the sign down? No, bollocks to that. Why should she be grateful when the estate agents were completely in the wrong. Sam had paid for supper. Should Dinah drop him a line to say thank you or what? Had she better scoop up the baby and take her into the big bed in case she got ill in the night? No, she'd kick, slew sideways, her hair would tickle and tomorrow would be hell as neither of them would have slept properly.

By now Dinah was in the bathroom, wondering who had nicked her toothbrush. Her skin looked dreadful and her legs really ached. She must remember to buy some moisturiser. Why had the baby put that flannel over her knee? Dinah got it at last. Sore knee, make it better. The 'make it better' was a command ordering the sopping poultice-type flannel to cure the graze and wasn't directed at her mother at all. Everything did make sense, thank God, and Dinah was a halfway decent parent after all. She was, she was, she was. Bugger her son's maths. She could decipher her two-year-old who almost certainly had not been poisoned, and she would engage with all homework in future, she really would, and her son wouldn't know what had hit him. She'd been taken out to dinner and she'd been raped twenty-five years ago and fairly recently she'd been traded in by her long-term partner, but she was okay. Yes, she could do it.

The compartments were back in place with almost no sloppage. Dinah subsided into bed. Things had been slipping a bit at work recently, but tomorrow she'd get on in there and kick arse and delegate effectively. Actually, perhaps she would go and look at the baby after all, just to be on the safe side. No, she was too tired to move. She couldn't decide. Hell. Finally Dinah hauled herself upright and stumbled back downstairs to check on all three children, inadvertently kicking over the dregs of her tea as she went.

Pain

TINA HAD always been going to have children. It was part of her make-up as far as she was concerned, like her eye colour or her middle name; so much so, in fact, that she'd never given it a lot of thought. Placidly she'd gone through the motions: a good school, a couple of modest trips abroad with girlfriends, a degree, followed by a brief period messing about in badly paid publishing jobs. In reality, though, she had always been soft-pedalling, just waiting for the squeaky cellophane to be twisted off the rock, a bright chunk bitten clear and the writing inside revealed for all to see. Good Mother.

Tina had pretty hazel eyes flecked with gold, creamy skin and a neat little mouth and nose. Morbidly conscious of her plump calves, she invariably wore designer jeans, teamed with court shoes and pastel blouses. Confidently, at twenty-seven, she took her first big stride in the direction of her life proper when she met and married Jonty Bellamy. Jonty worked in the City like most of Tina's circle, and was big and bluff with a brickish complexion. Strawberries and cream, he used to say, clutching Tina's fingers in his big red paw. Tina's parents, retired and aching for grandchildren, had finally sold the big old house near Guildford that Tina and her brother had grown up in and moved to an ugly bungalow. It was on a new estate, but uncomfortably close to their old house, in Tina's view. From the combined and advantageous sales of their previous flats, and with an additional boost from her parents, Tina and Jonty were able to buy a modest house in Fulham, albeit with a large mortgage.

Jonty had been pretty relaxed about if, when and how he and Tina would have children, so initially it was all driven by her. He loved her, though, and started to dread the ongoing misery over her repeated failure to conceive. He hated seeing her gusted about by the disappointment and thrown off track. It wasn't supposed to be this difficult, he thought ruefully, wondering how best to rally her. Once her period was a few days late, just the once. It had arrived with a vengeance before she'd felt confident enough even to buy a pregnancy test, but given the otherwise clockwork regularity of her cycle almost down to the hour, this tiny non-event had given her hope for a while.

Then, as they hit their early thirties, Jonty started to rue their childlessness as well. He found the state of it socially draughty and felt exposed by the lack of plant. There should have been booster seats in the car by now and brightly coloured plastic slides out on their lawn. For the first time ever, Jonty noticed himself becoming tense around his nephews and nieces as, knocking about at family events, they refracted his own lack back at him in a way that made him uncomfortable and moody. Up till now he'd thought of himself as an easygoing sort of a cove. In the past, in the main, everything had gone to plan: a decent job, a pleasant house and a presentable spouse. Why was this next phase eluding him?

Tina wanted a baby quite desperately now. She craved it bunched up inside her, wriggling about in her belly, and each bloody month the absence hurt her more. She felt victimised by everything, from little bath ducks in her local chemist to radio programmes about the growing incidence of anorexia in adolescent boys. Detail, thought Tina fiercely. I wouldn't mind a horrifically thin or a woefully fat child if I had one at all. Just one baby growing nicely and calmly inside me. Although Tina was stalked by beakers with spouts and little nursery lamps, she couldn't actually imagine the baby outside of herself, living in the world at large and benefiting from such items. As it couldn't seem to get started, it was hard to imagine it finished, and, try as she might, she really could not envisage that imaginary baby as something separate from her.

Jonty, on the other hand, just wanted children generally, around and about. He was hazy with regard to the detail, and on the rare occasions that he tried to focus on what precisely he was missing, he could only come up with a composite amalgam of children from ads. Sugar-pink daughters might be nice, he supposed, in charming sleepwear when he got back from work, or keen little sons with freckles kicking balls into fold-up goals he'd bought for them at Homebase. Children would form an undemanding frieze around the edges of his life, a pleasing backdrop. Tina's one imaginary baby never left her womb, whereas Jonty could only ever anticipate them in the plural, ready-made with a range of ages and hairstyles. The pair of them were too superstitious to discuss names openly but privately Jonty favoured Elizabeth, Henry and George, whereas Tina simply could not settle on the one perfect and all-encompassing name for a girl or boy. Nothing was quite right enough.

Eventually they went to the clinic. They should have gone before, but had been stubbornly resisting it as a depressing admission to each other and the world in general that there was a problem in this key area of their lives. And it was him. Well, more him than her, at least: not many sperm and all of them more or less inert. Jonty was sensible enough to know that it shouldn't matter, but found, unsurprisingly, that it pissing well, fucking well, bloody well did. Stupidly he'd been a bit public about the tests, which didn't help. Poor old Tina, he owed it to her, he supposed. I wanted to be supportive and all that. And now? Firing blanks, old chap? That had to be one of the most hateful expressions ever, and as an acknowledgement of a mortifying condition, it stung him like a slap. What should they do? The notion of donor sperm appalled him, obviously, and they knew instinctively that their relationship couldn't accommodate adoption, especially of the kinds of kids that might be available to them if magazine articles were to be believed. They wondered, they worried and they both got progressively more stressed.

After another consultation they were told that there was a slim chance that Jonty's few lively sperm could be separated out and injected directly into Tina's eggs. If it worked, a maximum of three fertilised eggs could be transferred back into her womb. Perhaps? Maybe? The technology was being refined all the time. They decided to go for it and embarked almost immediately on the whole undignified, time-consuming and emotionally draining shebang.

Jonty found it unbearable. Invasive was the word. It was horribly invasive. Tina, though, was pleased to be addressing things at last. That was the spar she clung to through the physical battering to which she was subjected – taking hormones, having her eggs harvested and so on – but as time went on she too became progressively disheartened. The procedures induced savage headaches, weight gain and mad mood swings, but still she couldn't get pregnant. The fertilised eggs wouldn't take.

Somehow Tina wasn't surprised, and, alongside the

searing disappointment, felt oddly vindicated by her continued failure to achieve a pregnancy. She had, of course, started to feel fatalistic about her chances, largely to protect herself, but also because the institutional nature of the proceedings surrounding each sad little failed attempt debilitated her. It was a vicious circle. If all the energy was being drained from her like this, how would she ever be able to muster the resources to protect and nourish these putative babies in the way that she felt she ought? Everything about her need had become so complicated.

Tina's misery was then further exacerbated by a perverse rash of pregnancies breaking out all around her. Suddenly she couldn't move for bumps, styled more and less successfully, and didn't even seem to be safe from women who she thought had had all their children. Abi was a typical example. She was a few years older than Tina, their mothers had been friends, and they had often ended up catching the bus to school together. Tina had always felt invested in Abi's career, getting a buzz from Abi's meteoric rise up the Civil Service. She knew that Abi had had her daughters quite young – Bea and Alice; nice names, Tina thought, filing them away – and she had certainly made more of her life overall than Tina had. Abi had been head girl as well, highly organised and smart – fast-stream, in fact, and something of a star. So when the tabloids' suspicions about the precise nature of Abi's relationship with that young black journalist started to seep out, Tina did feel slightly smug. Apparently even a well achieved life could fly off the rails unexpectedly, and it was all so public.

Intrigued, Tina started to look out for Val's pieces in the press. The way in which he tackled his subject matter seemed to her rather left-wing, but then she supposed that being a refugee might affect the way in which you viewed the world. Sitting down and grappling with his articles, she found to her surprise that his writing was more accessible than she'd feared, and oddly persuasive. He was an extremely attractive man. The little snapshots at the top of some of his articles didn't really do him justice, but he'd been on telly a couple of times, once arguing with Abi, and his easy charm, charisma even, shone out of their dusty little screen. Tina tried to imagine what it might be like kissing him or being made love to by him, but couldn't easily make that mental leap. Abi was certainly less attractive than him, but she carried herself well and had always had oodles of confidence.

The rumours about their involvement with each other seemed to fizzle out over that summer, and eventually the tabloids lost interest. Abi had managed to hold on to her job, too. Well, you couldn't sack someone for possibly having had sex with someone they shouldn't have, or who wasn't officially their current partner, could you, really?

Tina had determined to forget about Abi and all of that for a while. She had thought that to keep scrutinising other women's lives in close-up like this might be detrimental to her own hopes of achieving a pregnancy; she was trying to focus exclusively and productively on her own life. One lunchtime, though, folding clean newspaper to go under the cat's bowl, her eye was caught by a dull-looking supplement with a photograph of Abigail Howard on its front page. She was visiting a new benefits office on the Isle of Wight and, to Tina's admittedly obsessive eye, looked bulky. It could just have been the cut of her winter coat, as the photograph was grainy and Abi small in it overall.

Tina sighed, gritted her teeth and rang her mum. The two mothers, Pamela and Janice – equally awful names, thought Tina irritably – had stayed close and still played bridge and golf together. Did she know? Had she heard?'

'What, Tina?'

Had Abi, was Abi . . . ?

'Oh, I thought I'd mentioned it . . .'

They both knew she hadn't, for fear of upsetting Tina, who had, after all, been 'trying' for quite some time now. Tina hadn't told her mother about the treatment, as whatever her mother's reaction – and Tina couldn't be sure which way she would go on this one – it wouldn't be worth it overall.

'Yes, Janice told me in Marks's. Quite funny, really. We were both after the same grey turtleneck and grabbed it from opposite sides of the whotsit.'

You are a grey turtle, thought Tina. That tiny head

with its helmety grey perm shoots forward, beady eyes swivelling for any details that you can savour or use against me while appearing not to.

'Whose is it?' enquired Tina boldly, boosted by finally identifying the creature her mother reminded her of. She must remember to tell her brother next time he rang. Unfortunately he was the only other person in the world who would really get it, see how one-hundred-per-cent brilliantly apposite it was. She could try Jonty, but it wasn't really his thing, and besides, he'd always found her mum okayish, as possible mothers-in-law went. 'Well, you know, darling one, she is clean, compos and pretty independent. What more could one hope for realistically?' Compassion, thought Tina blackly; compassion and a smidgeon of humour, for starters. The list is endless frankly, Jonty, old thing, but never mind.

'Tina, did you just ask me whose baby it was? Well how on earth do you expect me to know something like that? Janice did mention that Abi had moved into a little studio – is that what you call it? – round the corner, you know, to be near the girls, as Alice is still quite young. Janice feels more comfortable with her younger granddaughter. I don't think Bea is exactly "on message", whatever that means.' Pamela paused briefly for effect. 'Paul has always been very capable, had to be, really, didn't he, poor chap, the hours Abi worked and the girls elected to stay with him, apparently. Perhaps Abigail is "seeing", as you young

euphemistically seem to describe it these days, someone else. How should I know? That black chap's back
with his girlfriend. She's pregnant as well, according to
Janice, and Abi's very pleased for them. They were
only ever friends and the press got it all out of
proportion, apparently.'

'Mum, are you wearing that mauve tweed skirt?'

'Tina, are you feeling quite all right?'

'Yes, I'm fine. I suddenly had a blindingly vivid
picture of you in that skirt, sitting in the armchair by
the television, and I just wanted to check.'

Tina put the phone down, feeling dizzy. She wanted
to cry. Babies wherever you looked and of all colours,
it seemed. The skirt enquiry had just been a decoy.
Thankfully it had stopped her mother dead in her
tracks, not an easy thing to achieve on an endless
Thursday afternoon. So, Abi was pregnant again. In
spite of her manic resolution only to focus on herself
at the moment, Tina knew from experience that she
couldn't hide from the pain of an unfair fact as horribly
hurtful as this one. It would just haunt her, jumping
out mockingly when she was feeling tired, or low
about the apparent impossibility of ever managing to
have children of her own. No, she needed to think
about this particular baby compulsively, a bit like
chewing on a difficult bit of meat, and then gradually
it might lose its power to upset or choke her.

One day, when the endless hideous processes and
appointments had been preoccupying them both for

months, Jonty, to his surprise, found himself above a dry cleaner's in Cricklewood. On what he was sure was a whim, he'd phoned a number that had jumped out at him from a small and relatively upmarket men's magazine. This magazine had been lying around in the bar at his squash club, had somehow found its way into his sports bag and then into his car, and then the number had got written into his address book, half at the front and half in the middle – not, of course, that he'd ever ring it. He and Tina were fine. Sex was bound to be a bit rocky with all these fertility worries flying around; bound to be, everyone knew that. Even before all of this recent assisted malarkey, the pressure of trying had taken a lot of the fun out of sex, for him, anyway.

Still, now, walking up the second flight of stairs, he couldn't quite believe he'd found both bits of the number, dared to ring it and made an appointment. At the edges of his psyche, buried quite deep, there had always been a desire to push out the boundaries of his wholesome sexual encounters with Tina, but his occasional clumsy signals had been met with confusion. Then when, self-consciously, he had become a little more explicit, his vague hopes had been instantly dashed with, 'Don't be a silly, Jonty,' from Tina. 'We're not perverts yet,' followed by a tinkly laugh that verged on the hysterical to show how broadminded she was really. *Broad*-minded! He guffawed to himself, feeling confident and American suddenly. This woman wouldn't know, wouldn't care about babies, sperm, the whole damn production that sex, his and Tina's future, most flaming aspects of his life, seemed to have become recently; although it wasn't a production, of course, as it appeared that they couldn't produce. Chrissake! Why did his brain keep punning back at him like this? Nerves, he supposed. Of the two of them, Tina was the one who liked words, books, dragging him off to the National to see God knows what . . . Tina, Christ! He didn't want her sweet, blunt little face dancing about in his mind's eye as he rang this particular bell.

Jonty hadn't known what to expect, but none of the things he had worried about in advance would trouble him the next time now that he'd done it and knew the form. Was there going to be a next time? Yes certainly. It had been exciting, hadn't hurt anyone, and no one need ever know. Everything there, in her spacious den, premises – he couldn't quite think of the right word to describe it – was scrupulously clean and well organised, and Jonty relished the fact that the non-judgemental transaction had been so impersonal. He was intrigued to observe that both his pleasure during the processes and his subsequent relief didn't seem in any way to be tied up with what the woman looked like. That's why it had felt distinct from all the other sexual encounters he'd ever had. In the past he'd only ever been turned on by women who attracted him physically in some way – voice, hair, gestures, it didn't matter what the trigger was, but there always had to have been that starting point. This woman looked smart and efficient, wore some pretty exciting variants on themes he'd barely ever dared even acknowledge to himself as erotic, but there was nothing about her physicality that chimed with his desires. She did seem to know exactly where and how much to hurt him, though, and he thrilled to the different experiences and sensations.

He never made love to her, that wasn't what it was about at all, but the etiquette and related signals buried deep within the pretence of it all were so clear, and yet so subtle, that he felt utterly safe and happy being led around the various stimulating landscapes that she had on offer. Initially he had been quite shy, but then, as his feelings of guilt and embarrassment diminished and his confidence grew, he began to participate in the set-ups more actively, indicating what aroused him or what he'd like to try next. Slowly he discovered what he enjoyed most and what pleasures he must have dreamed of without their ever having crystallised clearly in his imagination before. None of it was particularly outlandish. He liked being beaten, being verbally abused, particularly when she was wearing spikily high-heeled shoes, and he liked the feeling of thin rubber or clingwrap stretched tightly over his skin. Their exchanges before and after the show, as he started to think of it, were carefully limited on both sides and he liked that as well. There was no nightmarish pretence about being friends. After each session he would replay the sequence back to himself repeatedly, often during dullish meetings, until the pleasurable bite of the memory slowly lost its power to thrill him. Then, after a decent interval, two or three weeks maybe, he'd make another appointment.

Late one afternoon, when, cautiously, he rang his dominatrix from the office, planning, as he punched in the numbers, the things he'd get her to do to him later that week, her number didn't engage. He tried again but it seemed to be out of order or malfunctioning in some way. How maddening. He realised then how much he'd been counting on seeing her in the next couple of days. The incidence of his visits had been creeping up slightly, a fact he was managing to gloss over to himself by being super-patient with Tina's largely hormone-induced truculence. Eventually he went round to Cricklewood, but she'd gone, clearly. The attic door was locked, and there was a drift of manky pizza flyers up against it. Jonty had liked her and trusted her and didn't have the heart or know-how to find anyone else, so that was that. For good or bad, though, it had opened tiny portholes inside him that he knew he would never be able to snap shut again entirely. It wasn't the fact of doing it, but the fact of having done it.

Jonty wondered if what he'd been up to, spreading hair-crack fissures through his marriage, would at any level have been registered by Tina. It was impossible to tell, as everything had become so tricky between them. This pregnancy imperative was corroding normality to such a degree that it was unlikely that Tina could have noticed anything specifically different with regard to sex – his lack of appetite, or even the hiding of odd marks and bruises from her. In fact, given everything that was currently going on with her body, normal sex with each other had seemed unwise, boat-rocking, even. Was it possible, Jonty wondered, that he had been stained, even so, in a way that he couldn't see or recognise, but that Tina could somehow sense? If infidelity was a flight away from your present, your primary existence, would it ever be possible to return comfortably to where you'd left off when it was finished?

Jonty wasn't used to thinking in this way, about things that existed but that you couldn't see. 'I'm a take-life-as-it-comes kind of a bloke' he'd always protested if something in his life ever demanded even a smidgeon of introspection or forward planning. The notion of subsidence had lodged in his head now, though, with regard to his marriage and he couldn't expel it. Surely they would have to acknowledge the cracks eventually? How, he wondered to himself on the tube, did you underpin a marriage if you had different sexual tastes and if you couldn't have children? Therapy? That was out of the question. The word alone made him feel as though he was wearing a nappy in public. Anyway, he still loved Tina. He was worried about things between them, certainly, but talking about it to a stranger, rather like adopting someone else's child, just wouldn't ever be possible for him. Besides, he and Tina hadn't even acknowledged the existence of any problem to each other yet – well, beyond the crushing, overwhelming lack-of-baby issue, of course.

Maybe there was no problem. It didn't seem fair, given her understandable and all-consuming getting-pregnant preoccupation, to load anything else on to her at the moment. If they did manage to have a kid, kids, unimaginable though it all seemed currently, that would surely blast away these indefinable abstract worries he'd been having post his secret Cricklewood assignations. But what if they didn't have children and his worries got worse? What if they had been fine, up to a point, the pair of them, living fairly comfortably in, or rather on, their marriage, which recently he'd started to see as a cosy small rug.

Christ, it was so hard to express, but he was determined to try and make sense of this, for himself, at least. Maybe he and Tina could pull through and no one would ever know that he'd had doubts about the whole bloody marriage thing. Maybe not even Tina would suspect anything, if he could only think it all through calmly to some sort of a conclusion. So where was he? Yes. There was this piece of plain carpet which was their marriage; serviceable, comfortable carpet, which recently he'd ventured off to try out some yellow linoleum instead. He didn't want to live on the yellow linoleum, but equally, he didn't want to rule it out for the rest of his life. He knew that if he could achieve a safe sexual context like Cricklewood had been to experiment in, then he would welcome the possibility of exploring different colours and textures of floor coverings. What if he found someone who was cautiously interested in experimenting with him who wasn't a prostitute? Someone he fancied like Tina – well, not like Tina, obviously. How would that be?

Jonty poured himself a hefty whisky and paced about some more. He'd told Tina he'd be up shortly, just had a bit of work to finish, and she was fine with that. She understood when he needed his space. In lots of ways they fitted together nicely. That was the devil of it. Money? Houses? How would all that work out if everything did blow up, or more probably slowly slide into total disrepair when no babies were forthcoming. Strangely, he found that he wasn't scared of that side of things. Anyway, he really, really couldn't do anything about these doubts at the moment. As Jonty took his glass through to the kitchen, the phone rang, which was bloody odd at ten to midnight. It was Tina's dad, who didn't want Tina disturbed, but just wanted them to know that her mum was going into hospital the next day. He was whispering from the lounge after Pamela had finally gone up to bed. Jonty was thrown by the wretched symmetry of it – wives in bed, husbands downstairs wrestling with imponderables.

In the event, Pamela was discovered to have a large tumour which was classified inoperable by her oncologist. Tina categorically refused to engage with this situation, and placid, easygoing Jonty was quite shocked. He rang regularly and drove down by himself for Sunday lunch with his parents-in-law, taking them a carefully chosen plant for their minuscule garden, all in the absence of any concern or even input from his wife. Tina couldn't easily explain the intensity of her revulsion even to herself. It was something odd to do with the fact her mum was growing a lump, and, ridiculous though it seemed, Tina was convinced that any exposure to it might somehow harm her own prospects. Absurd, superstitious, almost deranged, in fact, but she knew that she just couldn't help herself and categorically refused to be anywhere near her mother physically or emotionally just now.

Each time the supposedly fertilised eggs were implanted, Tina would feel stupidly protective of her stomach. She'd walk upstairs oh so cautiously to avoid jolting the little chaps trying to grow inside her. She envisaged them as tiny scraplets, the size of peas, that mustn't be jiggled about or they could lose their grip and tumble out. Tina withdrew into her own head, trying to focus, trying to cook a baby inside her with surging, warming, nourishing thought-waves. She even avoided walking down streets where there were roadworks in case the thumping pounder things affected her insides with their vibrations and dislodged the babies.

Finally, and on what she and Jonty had agreed would be their last attempt at this method, Tina seemed to stay pregnant. Two of the little fertilised eggs managed to hang on inside her and she found that almost more difficult to negotiate than losing them had been. Each day that she woke up, not in any pain and not bleeding, neurotically listening to her stomach for any unusual or alarming sensations, she felt happy and anxious, hysterical and hopeful in the most exhausting combinations. Eventually her consultant told her that she should start to tell people that she was pregnant with twins and that way she might be able to stop mentally clutching wood and start to believe in this pregnancy as a reality.

Jonty, steady and supportive throughout, cautiously mooted a trip down to his in-laws to tell them the news in person, and to his surprise Tina agreed. As they hadn't been told about the treatment, the pregnancy could even be presented as a normal, unassisted success, and rather helpfully there was a history of twins in the family.

Tina's mother was a bad colour when they arrived, and in quite a bit of pain, but she'd still managed a good spread. She appeared thrilled with their news and everyone tiptoed carefully round the painfully ugly central issue of whether or not the births would precede the death. As he sipped his sherry, Jonty's head was whirling with it all. Was it possible that, against all the odds, Tina's mum might outwit her terminal cancer, or that both twins could still die before they'd been born? Now that children were more than a possibility, and even though they were still terrified of losing them, it was already becoming hard to remember with any precision the intensity of their recent yearnings. It didn't make sense to him. Tina had been desperate for kids, but since getting pregnant had become wholly indifferent to her own mum. What if, when she had kids, they ignored her when she got ill and needed them? Maybe that wasn't what it was about. But then what was the point of all this? Whichever way you looked at it, the whole life cycle thing was baffling.

They had to stop at a service station on the relatively short drive home so that Tina could go to the loo. Before Jonty could open his door and get round to help her out, Tina put her hand on his leg and asked him if he thought they'd get through all of this.

Jonty was confused. 'All of what? Your mum's illness? Managing twins after having waited for so long? What exactly do you mean?'

'I don't know,' she said, and then, 'no, don't get out, darling. It's cold and I'm sure I can manage.'

She heaved herself out of the car and trundled over to the nasty burger place to look for the loos. Jonty felt both protective and wistful watching her normal-sized back in its maroon winter coat diminish away from him through the passenger window.

Tina was already so bulky and awkward that she opted for the wheelchair loo with the big chrome handles to pull herself up and down on. Abi's mum had been to see her mother, which was nice. She'd brought a big bunch of orange chrysanthemums and a picture of Abi's toddler, Jack, who was white. Not, of course, that there had ever been any doubt about that. Abi's mum was worried that Abi was a bit lonely living alone with Jack, but she had her career, she supposed. The girls were both doing well, although, confidentially, Bea did seem to have a wild streak where boys were concerned. Paul had a nice new girlfriend who worked for a charity, the girls seemed to like her, and they were going to get married in the spring. Abi's mum was intrigued about whether or not she'd be invited to the wedding. Not hung up about it, she stressed to Tina's mum, just intrigued. 'Everything's so different these days isn't it? One can be at a bit of a loss I find. I've always got on with Paul, though, and the girls are still my grand-daughters.'

There was Abi, with an impressive career and a third baby, but a bit isolated and out in the cold, and here was Tina, about almost to catch up by having two babies at once, without a job, with a dying mother, which only made her feel bad because she didn't feel worse about it, and a decent, dependable husband, who in some strange way she felt as though she'd lost along the way.

He'd gone missing a couple of months ago. That was an odd thought, wasn't it? It was the first time Tina had even begun to acknowledge the possibility of changes in their relationship, while knowing at the same time that it was clearly absurd. It had to be the hormones. Had to be. Jonty was as keen as she was to compare double buggies, for heaven's sake, and had already decorated the spare room in lemon paint with a dear little clown border. Adding it all up, she supposed that overall she was better off than Abi at this moment, but it was hard to say. Why, she wondered, did women always do that? Compete across such a ridiculously wide spectrum of so-called achievements without ever even acknowledging to each other or themselves that calculating and comparing like this was a lifelong preoccupation.

Jonty was standing by the bonnet of the car, smoking and looking anxious.

'You were hours, and I didn't know what to do. Wasn't sure about the propriety of standing outside the girls' lav, shouting for you.'

Tina smiled. His description conjured up a chintzy boarding school but hardly covered the grubby cubicle that she'd been collapsed in, daydreaming.

'Sorry, Jonty. Everything seems to take me ages at the moment.'

He dropped his cigarette on to the tarmac and kicked it out.

'I know I shouldn't be smoking, but I thought maybe you wouldn't mind. It has been a hell of a day, for one reason and another, and you're pretty solidly preggers by now.'

They got back into the car, two adults with two babies inside one of them, with Tina reflecting that Jonty was solicitous, protective and had been more than patient with regard to her recent weird behaviour over her mum. He was driving, he was in charge, he'd be there at the birth, but maybe soon he wouldn't be around anymore. Lovers, babies, parents, tumours. They configured themselves in the oddest combinations and in patterns that you could never really anticipate.

Tina looked sideways at her husband's familiar profile and then forward at the motorway unrolling ahead of her. As she rummaged in the glove compartment for the old-fashioned tin of glucose-dusted sweets, she decided that she would simply try and take things as they came, and for the moment, at least, she felt content to do so.

Goodbye For Ever

ALEX WOULD always remember every detail of the interminable afternoon he spent hunched in his crappy old Renault in a vast car park, picking at the lace of the nasty leatherette steering wheel cover which he loathed but had never removed. Grubby litter blew about in mini-cyclones, the grey concrete vista was splotched with old oil stains and there were only a couple of other cars beside his, empty, apologetic and huddled in close.

He'd taken Mandy into the building earlier, unsure whether to carry her bag or what, exactly. They weren't lovers any more and they certainly weren't friends. It was one of those situations where circumstances bind together two people who rightfully should be miles apart. This time round she had seemed pretty certain about the procedure, operation – they weren't nice words, any of them. Mandy could still bolt, though, knowing her. She still had time. Fuck, fuck, fuck, quite literally.

Alex banged his forehead down on the steering wheel. It hadn't seemed right to hang about in the grim floral reception area, but he would do anything – well, almost anything – to make sure that this time she saw it through. Mandy knew that she had him back in her power, and for weeks he'd been hooked like a helpless wriggling fish. She'd summoned him over to hers endlessly after work, which had taken for ever in the rush-hour traffic, and on the evenings that he didn't go, there were always lengthy phone calls into the small hours. He had tried to placate her without sending out the wrong signals, but it had been an impossible situation, and Alex felt as though he'd been living in the frightening dark tunnel of it now for ever.

Mandy and he had split up months ago, and it had been ugly and badly handled, and he did acknowledge that now, but at the time he hadn't realised that there'd been anything at stake. The split had been coming for a while, in his mind anyway, but had been precipitated by Mandy's admission that she'd been to those school-uniform discos a couple of times. 'Just a bit of fun. What's your problem? And I look really good in the gear.' A short grey skirt with those absurd legs, Alex could imagine, and he still got an erection at the thought. Christ, though, she was a mother, and these fantasies had seemed to him tacky and desperate. You were supposed to move forward in life, weren't you? Wasn't that the point of growing up? When he gave it a bit more thought, he realised that this pretty harmless detail typified his problems with Mandy generally. She got off on behaving like a child or adolescent, and was irrational and spoilt, refusing, it seemed to him, to live anywhere but in the immediate present. He didn't feel as though he was inappropriately obsessed with income, pensions or any of that stuff, but by the time he was Mandy's age he would hope to have achieved a mortgage somehow, a promotion perhaps, and ideally a serious relationship. He sensed vaguely that before too long he would need more than just great sex from a girlfriend.

Alex had badly bitten fingernails and a soft white body in spite of erratic attendances at the gym, but was attractive enough, with spiky gelled hair and an impish grin. He had acquired Mandy without too much effort, so it seemed likely that he would get someone else, someone better, soon enough. Well, his mates assured him he would, round at his over pizzas when he'd got in all the beers.

After the split, Alex felt as though he had put Mandy behind him and moved on. He worked as an accountant for a company that manufactured toys and old-fashioned children's clothes. It was based in a featureless industrial unit in Acton and as if to compensate for this, the sales catalogue featured cute line drawings of tiny cottages and windmills linked with humped-back bridges. This biscuit-tin landscape was interspersed with photographs of the products, smocked party dresses and wooden-handled skipping ropes. The customers were all buying into a fictional past as well, but that didn't trouble Alex in quite the same way as the thought of Mandy and her girlfriends queuing outside clubs in school uniform. It was a modest enough job, but a good one for someone at his stage, and he took it seriously. He fancied Daisy the receptionist and had asked her out a couple of times in a group with some of his mates.

On the afternoon when Mandy rang up a couple of months after they had split up and he wasn't at his desk, Daisy gave him the message. She told him that Mandy had been sobbing. Alex liked the fact that Daisy was worried and sisterly rather than what's-her-problem-stupid-cow, but on that particular day he was up against it with mountains of year-end paperwork and just couldn't face the stress, emotional blackmail, whatever it was going to turn out to be. In the end he didn't return her call. He felt bad briefly, but not for long. They had split up, after all, and Mandy did have family around if there was some kind of crisis. He couldn't stay on hand in her life just to sort out her DVD player or comfort her if someone had been horrid to Jess. It wasn't helpful. Jess wasn't his child, and Mandy needed to move on as well. Alex got a watery hot chocolate from the office vending machine to buck himself up and dived back into his spreadsheets.

When finally he left work it was quite late, maybe seven or so, and Mandy was waiting by his car. Alex's heart sank, knowing it must be heavy shit if she'd got a babysitter for Jess. She looked tired, bitter somehow, and there was no preamble.

'I'm pregnant.'

His heart did an aching double-thump.

'What?'

'You heard me.'

'Yup. Yup.' Alex said it twice as if jauntyness could ward off the horror. 'Hop in.'

He got in himself and leaned across to open the passenger seat as it always needed a bit of a shove, but she seemed unsure. Barelegged, she dithered about, frowning and clutching her doll-size bag to her chest with both hands.

'Get in, for God's sake,' Alex barked. 'I'm not going to bite.'

Still she wouldn't get into the car and then she started to cry. Clearly, tetchiness was unproductive so he got out and put his arm round her. She shrugged him off and started petulantly to kick at one of his front tyres.

'I wasn't going to tell you, actually.'

Why have you, then, he wondered, his annoyance gathering momentum; the tyre was bald and he couldn't afford a new one just now.

'You can't claim benefit if you don't say who the dad is, so I'll have to tell them.'

'What? Jesus Christ. What are you telling me? You're not going to have it, are you? Don't be ridiculous, Mand! You've already got one.'

'Don't you dare talk about Jess like that. I hate you.'

Mandy turned and tottered off awkwardly in her

heels, one arm flailing out for balance and the other clutching her tiny bag. She looks like a mad baby giraffe, thought Alex sadly. What am I going to do? She can't have it. She just can't. There's no point. We're not together any more and it would be a disaster for both of us.

Mandy rang him later that evening, ricocheting between tears and anger. She reckoned that she was already about fourteen weeks, agreed with him that she couldn't possibly have this baby and raise it by herself, and then almost immediately changed her mind. They both knew that she was angling for them to get back together, but Alex was already far beyond that. Meticulous about contraceptives, he supposed the condom must have burst, but months later it was hard for him to remember any particular occasion when that might have happened. Once, in the middle of the night, he remembered that he'd slipped on a knotted rubber by the bed when he went for a slash, and on another occasion he'd been grossed out when he had found a fluorescent orange one floating in the dregs in a coffee mug. He tried and tried to think back and woke up spinning at four in the morning wondering what he'd done to deserve this nightmare scenario, desperate to wind the clock back and rewrite his own history.

At that stage, Mandy had been looking for somewhere cheap to rent. She was in the process of extricating herself from her husband, and sometimes, when he was away on business, she and her daughter used to stay over. Six-year-old Jess worshipped Alex and his flatmate Pete. 'Boys!' she'd command, clapping her hands and pulling at them, 'play with me,' and they would, intrigued by this little girl gracing their ladsville squalor. A princess in pink pyjamas, she'd sit at their kitchen table, airily munching the fish fingers that her mum had brought in a small Tupperware box to heat up for her. Once she was settled in a makeshift bed in the passage and had been sung to rather raucously, Mand, Alex and sometimes Pete as well would eat takeaways, drink beer and get stoned.

It was good fun at first as Alex liked having Mand as a girlfriend, and Jess was a dear little added extra. He was tickled by her freckles, her snubby nose, and the way she put her knife and fork together emphatically when she'd finished eating. Once he bought her a miniature Lego car to assemble.

'But she's a girl,' whined Mandy.

'Yes, she's a girl. But you keep telling me that she's good at maths and her dad works with computers, doesn't he, so maybe she'll want to be an engineer or something.' Mandy went on sulking, probably irked by the mention of her husband, so Alex told her she looked stunning, which she did, and then kissed her energetically with a mouth full of cold beer, which made her giggle, and she stuck her hand down his jeans as an indication that she might just forgive him.

Alex had been told what time he could come back

to collect Mandy but had had to ask another three times as he kept forgetting to listen to the reply. The nurse, unmoved, was used to it. He'd felt sick with anxiety from the moment he had climbed back into his car, looking and looking at his watch, and then instantly checking it against the fuzzy square numbers on his free-with-oil dashboard clock. He couldn't read, couldn't listen to the radio, couldn't think, couldn't settle to anything, in fact. What if she'd changed her mind? He could not go through all this again. He just couldn't. He'd collapse pretending to like her, pretending to be sympathetic to the arguments, pretending he cared about Jess. No, that was the irony, actually. He liked Jess, he really did. He thought about her, worried about her, and missed her, even now, bustling self-importantly into the bathroom in the mornings with her princess sponge bag and sparkly toothbrush. He could picture that toothbrush so vividly lying on top of their cistern. Sometimes he even dreamed about Jess. That was weird, wasn't it, having a bossy little six-year-old lodged in his subconscious? Yeah, with a mother who dressed up in school uniform! Mandy was sexy, no doubt about it, but she just wasn't right for him.

Another seventeen seconds had passed according to the bleak dashboard figures.

From the moment he'd first met Jess, Alex had had a sense of her. He knew enough not to crowd her or try to impress her, but he also realised that it was important to acknowledge her. Somehow he had guessed that the key to gaining her trust might be asking her to chop carrots for lunch, and her mother had unwittingly played into his hands.

'Don't you think that knife's a bit sharp? It could easily slip, you know.' Mandy shook her head indulgently, smoothing down her dress as she recrossed her endless legs.

'She's fine,' Alex said soothingly, trying not to mind how many hours it would be before he could remove all of Mandy's clothes. 'Aren't you, Jess?'

And by saying that to her, she became even more careful, determined not to let herself down.

Jess had a brown fringe, brown eyes, and Mandy dressed her very simply, the girlie pyjamas and pink sponge bag being an exception. She usually wore denim pinafores with red tights, or jeans and checked shirts which charmingly underlined her practical bent. Oddly, neither Mandy nor Jess ever mentioned Vaughan, the supposedly unsatisfactory husband and father. Occasionally, when Jess wasn't around, Alex would press Mand to describe him, but she just crossed her eyes and grimaced. 'You don't want to know. You really don't.' Alex suspected the truth was pretty dull, and that Mandy wanted to make the marriage seem more eventful than it was, scary even. Her life was pedestrian enough in every other respect, and those dishonest dramatics were one of the many ways in which her immaturity manifested itself, he told himself pompously once they'd split up.

Mandy had already bolted from the clinic once. By then, Alex had been hashing over the rights and wrongs of an abortion with her non-stop for weeks and was already pretty near the end of his tether. He'd listened as patiently as he could while she'd circled round and round her queasiness that it wasn't right to have it removed simply because it didn't suit her to have another child at this stage. He had told her repeatedly that he wouldn't be there for either of them at any stage and wouldn't ever want to see the child. It was a tricky tightrope he had to walk, and there was never a moment's respite. If he was too brutal about his lack of interest, she would shut off and refuse to speak to him, but if he was kind and patient, he would sense the hope flaring up in her that they might get back together as a jolly family of four. Christ.

Finally the abortion had been agreed on, but Mandy had run away shortly after he'd left her in reception. She'd crashed out through a fire door, apparently, and although he hadn't actually seen her leave, he could easily picture her clattering off over the horizon, running away from the loss of this big new part of herself. Thank God she hadn't confided in Jess at any stage of the nightmare. That was one of the things that gave Alex hope that she might still end the pregnancy. This second time he was pretty sure that Mandy would go through with it. He didn't know why he thought that, he just had an instinct about it.

Comparing his watch with the dashboard clock for the millionth time, he paced around the car park a few times and finally went in to get her. Thankfully, she was there waiting for him as he lurched forward awkwardly, not quite sure which bit of her to touch or support.

Alex drove much more carefully than usual, stopping responsibly at orange lights and trying not to jolt her. Irrationally, he was frightened of breaking the moment, inadvertently reversing the procedure that had just taken place, and finding himself, snakes and ladders style, back at the start again with a stroppy pregnant Mand on his hands. As long as he drove sensibly, he hoped that time might continue to go forward properly, leaving their baby behind them in the past.

Back at Mandy's tiny flat above a gift shop, he helped her out of her coat and settled her on the sofa with her daughter's animal duvet and a cup of tea. He had to squash down a momentary pang at the photos of grinning, gap-toothed Jess dotted around the place, but otherwise felt okay. Surely he could decently leave now. There was nothing else that he could think of offering to do. It was a bit weird, though, that he would never see Mandy again, apart from bumping into her somewhere, but that was pretty unlikely as he lived in Battersea and she was now in North Finchley. He couldn't kiss her, obviously. What then? Just go? Friendly wave of the hand? She'd had an abortion, for

God's sake. Until a couple of hours ago they'd been linked physically by a scrap of flesh. More than just a scrap in fact . . .

For the very first time a tiny extra-terrestrial's baby face popped into his mind. It had been a nothing up till now, albeit an all-consuming one, but suddenly and ironically it had taken shape in his imagination at the very moment, presumably, that it was finally being flushed down some horrible hospital toilet or drain somewhere or burnt or put in a bin bag. What? What happened to them? He would never know where his daughter had been buried. Why did he think of it as a girl, suddenly? This was ridiculous. He should be feeling light as a feather. It had all finally happened. His life could unfreeze now, resume its usual momentum.

Mentally giving himself a shake, Alex gently touched Mandy's arm and said quietly, 'Well, I think I'll be making a move now.'

She rolled her eyes. 'What?'

He was defensive, jumpy, and the fact that she had finally done what he so desperately wanted her to do didn't seem to have caught up with his guts yet. They were still churning away. He felt anxious, tired and disgustingly sweaty. He thought he might faint.

'What is it?' Mandy was still a bit slurred. 'S'okay, buster. Don't panic. It's just what people say, isn't it? You know, "I think I'll make a move now." If they worry they're going to be made to stay or something. If it's too – what's the word – sudden, you know to say, "I'm off." Or, "Gotta go." Or just plain "Bye." It's okay, Alex, I won't kick up. I feel too rough.'

Surprised by her acuity, Alex suddenly felt affectionate. He bent down and brushed the hair from her face. 'I'll let you off seeing me to the door then, shall I?' But she barely looked back up at him, busy rummaging a celebrity magazine out of the bag she'd packed earlier for the clinic.

It was just about worth going back to work, but, conscientious as he usually was, Alex realised that he simply couldn't face anybody or anything more today. He was completely drained, but nervous and jittery as well. Even though he was awake and driving home against the traffic, for once, he felt as though he was dreaming. He and Mandy were running up a hill, swinging a little blob of foetus girl between them. She bounced between them and Jess danced about waiting for them to reach the top. 'What's that?' she screamed when she saw it. Next, the foetus grew fins out of the side of its head instead of ears and transformed itself into a miniature greyish-white seahorse. It dived into a suburban loo and down a peeling plastic drainpipe, but couldn't exit at the bottom as the end of the pipe was encased in metal.

Alex parked, shook his head in disgust and strode into the off-licence. Then, crossing back to his home and crashing the bottles down on to the path rather ill-advisedly, he started to search for his house keys with a bad feeling that got worse. He'd left them at Mandy's, by the kettle. No question. They were separate from his car key, and he'd been turning them over in his pocket all afternoon, trying and failing to break the skin on his thumb with them. He'd put them down by the kettle when he'd made Mandy tea. He remembered exactly how they'd looked on the sparkly grey worktop by the base of her plastic kettle. Alex slumped down lower on the doorstep. He hadn't got the heart to haul himself upright and go to the cinema or even the pub, although his flamate wouldn't be back for hours.

After a while the gate clicked and Alex looked up cautiously. It was the woman from the ground-floor flat with her toddlers asleep in their double buggy. He'd only spoken to her once, when the combination of shopping bags, tired children and a fiendishly narrow hall was defeating her and she'd been near to tears. Alex had never even noticed her husband.

She smiled at him. 'You okay?'

He stared at the ground, suddenly anxious that he in his turn might start to cry. She narrowed her eyes.

'Obviously not. Look, come in and have a cup of tea. I've got to feed these two in a bit, but they're quiet at the moment.'

Alex, turning his face still further away from her, managed a nod and struggled to his feet.

'Don't forget your shopping.'

Picking up his bag of booze, careful not to let it

clink too obviously, he followed her into the tidy living area. She put the kettle on and started to sort out baked beans and toast for her little boys. Alex took a breath.

'Please don't think badly of me, but I've had one of the worst days I've ever had in my life. I've mislaid my keys, and I really, really need a drink. Something stronger than tea, I mean. I've got some wine.'

The woman smiled. 'Why not? I think I can run to a corkscrew. I'm Tina, that's Jamie, and that's Sam.'

'Non-identical,' murmured Alex, squatting down by Sam, who was starting to stir. His experience with Jess had given him a bit more confidence with small children, even though he had rarely been exposed to them.

'Hi, cobber.'

'Cobb-bah,' said the child, putting his hand out for the bottle of wine.

Alex ripped the bright green foil off the cork and flicked it at him. The toddler giggled and batted it back as Alex held the bottle up behind his back for Tina to retrieve.

'I'm Alex, by the way.' Tina was getting glasses and opening the wine. 'What a good little chap. I expected him to be all crabby, waking up hungry and being confronted by a stranger. Up you go, fellah.' Sam, still transfixed by the crackly foil was content to be swung up by Alex and eased into his high chair.

The disjointedness of the grown-ups' exchanges as

Sam and then Jamie ate their beans, smeared them in their hair and made various demands on their mother, suited Alex perfectly. Earlier, slumped on the doorstep, he'd felt as though his personality, macerated by what he'd been through, had seeped away down a drain somewhere with his baby. Now, to his relief, tattered fragments of it seemed to be flying back into his possession. He tipped his wine down urgently, topping up Tina's glass, to her amusement, while it was still pretty full, before throwing himself whole-heartedly into mucking about with the boys while she ran them a bath.

'I better be off. Don't want your husband to feel usurped.'

'I haven't got one,' she shouted through from the bathroom. 'Well, not any more. Come on, lads! Bath time!'

The little boys didn't want to abandon the game, so Alex turned into a train and chuffed through into the bathroom. As he'd hoped, Sam and Jamie followed, intrigued, and their mother pounced on them and undressed them, laughing too loudly and joining in with the train noises. Her eyes were glistening with tears, which she rubbed away impatiently, and then, kneeling on the bathmat, tipping bath toys in on top of her sons, she looked up at Alex.

'We are a pair this evening, aren't we?'

He raised his eyebrows. 'Shall I go?'

'Only if you've had enough of us, which I would

quite understand, but please don't go on my account. We're enjoying the company, aren't we, small ones?'

Alex looked down at them. Did he want to go off upstairs and have those horrible dead-baby thoughts crowding in on him until he'd finally obliterated them with a lot more drink? Not really. Oddly, and this was really odd, he was having a nice time.

'Do you fancy an Indian?'

'What a good idea.' Expertly she hoiked Jamie out of the bath, removing the plug and swirling him in a towel before he noticed and protested. 'I was going to offer to make you something, but on reflection there's nothing nice to make and I haven't got the energy to improvise.'

Jamie had noticed that he was no longer in the bath whereas Sam was and started to wriggle and complain.

'They're getting tired.'

Alex whipped off his trainers and socks, hopped into the bath as the last bit of water swirled away and held out his arms for Jamie. 'Come here then, cobber.' He lifted him out of the damp towel nest on his mother's knee, sat him carefully on the rim of the bath and then slid him fast down and along, wheee, until he crashed into a startled Sam.

'Ghen. Ghen.'

'Okay, once more.'

'They'll want that every evening now,' said Tina, but she didn't mind. She was feeling unusually relaxed about everything, enjoying the wine on an empty stomach and the unexpected adult company. 'I'll just get their jim-jams'.

She reappeared with two sets of Pluto pyjamas and a twenty-pound note. 'Here. I'll settle them off if you get the food. Anything chicken and not too hot for me. I know it's a bit unadventurous, but I usually have a korma.'

'Cool.' Alex did an exaggerated thumbs-up for the boys. 'Okay if I stick some beers in the fridge?'

Everything meshed together neatly and the boys both went off to sleep with no fuss. Tina had a minor music trauma while Alex was out and in the end decided not to put anything on. He was probably fifteen years younger and would find her taste – which, rather like her cooking, she never seemed to get around to updating – middlebrow, naff, or, worst of all, would think she was trying to seduce him. How ghastly that would be just because she was an ageing single mum and he was being nice. But while she was sorting out plates and glasses after he'd got back he wandered over to her minisystem.

'D'you mind if I choose something?'

Tina shrugged nervously.

'Can't go wrong with Joanie. No, I've got it. Van. Perfect. That's just what I'm in the mood for.'

So that was that. What had all the fuss been about? Maybe she'd even get up the courage to tell him how she'd been singing along to 'I'm crazy for love but I'm not coming on' just as the cocky young washing machine repair man had arrived. Maybe she wouldn't.

'So, why was your day so crap?' She ripped her naan in half. 'God, I'm starving suddenly.'

Alex looked over at her. 'I will tell you what happened to me today, I promise I will but do you think you could go first? I'm having a nice time and I'll feel lousy again when I start talking about it. Why don't you tell me what happened to Jamie and Sam's dad and that'll give me the courage to tell you about this afternoon?'

'Okay, fair enough.'

Tina started talking, scraping at the edge of one of the foil dishes with her thumbnail.

'I did have a husband for a long time, and it was all fine and we had a nice house and very much wanted a family together, but it didn't happen and it didn't happen. In the end I went for a version of artificial insemination, and it still didn't happen, and then when it was almost too late for all sorts of reasons, it did eventually happen, but by then the marriage was over, give or take. It was quietly over, not with a loud bang or with other people being involved or anything, but still over, and we both just knew that it was. Now I've finally got my babes, but I just couldn't manage to have a husband and children together all at once in the way that it's supposed to happen.

'It was very hard for a while; awful, in fact. We had to sell up, and I had to swap my lovely house in Fulham for this little flat, and Jamie and Sam were so tiny. My mum died as they were born and, however weird this sounds, I sort of felt she'd done it on purpose. But it's okay now, although it's not the life I'd imagined and mapped out for myself. In fact, that was what a lot of the pain was about. Not all of it, but a lot. What I'd imagined I'd have as opposed to what I have ended up with! I still get teary when I see ads on telly for something stupid that I don't even want, like private health care. It's because they feature picture-perfect families with nice protective dads, a bit like Jonty was. They're actors in a fiction, though, and I do realise that now. Jonty adores Jamie and Sam, sees them regularly and gives us as much money as he possibly can. He's a nice guy, he really is, and I'm not sure what happened to us or what went wrong, apart, obviously, from the strain of all those procedures. They're horribly invasive, but conventional IVF wouldn't have worked for us. We had to have a special version where a single sperm is injected directly into each egg and then they're put back. Sorry, I'm running on rather.'

Alex shook his head. 'No you're not. It's fine. It's not something I know anything about.'

But his head was spinning again. Dear God! The lengths to which people had to go. Well, not Mandy, obviously.

'I wouldn't wish what happened to me on anyone – splitting up with Jonty, I mean,' continued Tina, gesturing at the remaining food. Alex shook his head again. She picked up the foil tray, deftly scooping up the remains of the rice with the last blistered fragment of naan. 'And it's not that I think nuclear families are crap or a waste of time. Not at all. But I was definitely wet before all of this happened, drifting along in my own little world and expecting big, strong Jonty to solve everything.'

Before that afternoon, Alex wouldn't have felt remotely equipped to listen to this kind of stuff, but after the steam-rollering he'd just gone through with Mandy, he found that he was intrigued by Tina's attempts to make sense of her past. He wriggled his bottom deeper into the seat to indicate that he was concentrating.

'A few good things have emerged from my marriage ending and my cosy little domestic pod being cracked open. I did have a pleasant life in the main, but I couldn't seem to stop obsessing about everything, turning inwards more and more, and obviously the difficulties in conceiving didn't help. I kept measuring myself against other women. How was I doing? Now I don't have the time for all that introspection, and I'm sure it's a healthier way to be.'

There was a sudden squawk from next door and Tina sprang up to check on the twins, but came back almost immediately.

'They're fine. Just a dream or something.'

Before she'd even sat back down she had picked up again.

'There's this woman I was at school with and always admired from a distance. She's much more of a career girl than me, a high-flyer in the Civil Service, has two teenage daughters but now she's alone with a baby too. We're going to meet up with the kids in the park one weekend. Well, that wouldn't have happened if I'd been with Jonty. I would still have been in awe of her. I'm rambling now. Sorry. No, I know that I am.'

Alex got the last beer out of the fridge by way of reply, snapped it open and split it between them. Clinking his glass against hers, he poked at the foam with his tongue before speaking.

'It must be tiring, though, working as well as looking after a pair of naughty toddlers.' He softened this with a smile as he didn't want her to think that he was being critical; the reverse, in fact, was true as he was still genuinely chuffed that she was confiding in him. The more she exposed herself, the keener he felt to protect her and make her feel safe within the conversation.

Tina took another big breath. 'Actually, I haven't admitted this to a soul as it's sometimes easier to seem hard done by, but I think, secretly, I prefer going out to work to looking after the twins day in, day out. Obviously I looked after them full time when they were born. I found it pretty nightmarish, actually, as there was no real differentiation between weekdays, weekends and holidays. Everything lumped itself together into a blur of tiredness. There was no respite, ever, which is an odd way, I know, to view pretty lowly office work. Of course I couldn't have worked if Jonty and I had stayed together as it would have seemed perverse, somehow, after all the hoops we jumped through to get our boys.'

'What is it that you do?' Alex asked.

Tina answered in a rush as if she was running out of time.

'I do a bit of proof-reading and run the office for a small publishing company.'

'Do you enjoy it?'

Tina smiled. 'Yes, I do. It's local and I really rate their books. It can be quite a thrill seeing the manuscripts in a state of undress one minute and then in shiny stacks in a bookshop the next. It's not unlike growing a baby, really, and then popping it out into the world for everyone to have a look at. Perhaps that's why I like it.'

Alex sighed inwardly. Did everything in the entire universe finally lead back to reproduction, he wondered wearily?

'I could get more money, perhaps, somewhere else, but I'd have to get buses and tubes and all of that. Oh, I don't know. For such a long time I so badly wanted to be a mother and have a child, and couldn't and couldn't. I was haunted by it and hated pregnant women as a result. I really hated them and wanted to smash them in the stomach with my fists and kick their babies to death in their tummies or steal babies from outside shops, as the mums leaving them there didn't seem to care enough about their good fortune. Occasionally I try to remember that phase and hug the children to me in my mind and hope that I am grateful enough, but of course it's frightening how quickly you start to take having them for granted as your absolute right. You can't go around all the time singing thank-you halleluiahs in your head, obviously, but maybe that's why I'm happy to potter along a bit at work for a while and mark time. I'm still superstitious, I think, about taking my eye off the ball with regard to my boys, failing to appreciate them fully and then somehow losing them.

'God, I'm sorry. I never talk this much, hog the conversation like this. Shut up, Tina. Tell me about your day. Please, I really want to hear what had been happening to you before I found you all caved in on the doorstep.'

Alex smiled and refused her as gently as he could.

'I couldn't after what you've told me. I just couldn't. It wouldn't be right.'

Tina shook her head in turn and started to cry.

'I'm sorry, I've been so rude. I've really been shockingly self-indulgent. I've never told anyone any of that stuff before. I don't know what's got into me. I don't feel as though I'm lonely, but maybe I am. Perhaps I've turned into one of those women without noticing: the ones who shout coo-ee all the time to people in the park who are just minding their own business and having a nice time with their families and wanting to be left in peace. You'll be scared that I'll leap out at you in the hall when you're going out in the evening. I've bored you. I know I have.'

Alex put his arm round her briefly before pulling her up from the table.

'You haven't bored me at all, I promise. Come and sit down for a moment.'

He led her over to the brick-brocade sofa and thought about sitting next to her, but decided against it as too intimate. The sofa was small and neat, designed for one and a half bottoms. He sat down on the floor instead, fairly close by.

'I promise that you haven't bored me. Are you free today week?'

Tina wiped her face with a corner of blouse, inadvertently affording him a glimpse of her milky stomach. She had a tiny dark mole on her side, and, unusually for him, he was neither aroused nor repulsed.

'Course I am.'

'Good. We can do this again, and that's when I'll tell you my story. You can get the wine and beers next time and I'll pay for the curry. How does that sound?'

He stood up, bent back down and kissed her cheek.

'And thanks for saving my evening. I would probably still be sitting out there morosely if you hadn't come back with your boys. They are great little lads, you know, and you're right to be proud of them.'

Tina jumped up to see him out. 'Sorry I talked about myself so much.'

Alex winked at her.

'Next time, I promise you, you won't get a word in edgeways.'

Conscious of Pete crashing about now above them, he ran upstairs and rapped on his own front door. His flatmate was clearly pissed. 'Where are your keys? Howdja get in downstairs?' There was a large scruffy girl behind Pete drinking coffee at their kitchen table and Alex felt weak.

'The woman in the ground-floor flat let me in.'

'Giving her one, were you? What is it with you and women with kids?'

Before Alex had even started to process Pete's remark properly, he grabbed his flatmate by the hair and slammed his head against the kitchen door. As Pete gulped and staggered upright, Alex, to his own surprise, and again before he really knew what he was doing, punched him in the face. Pete staggered against the door frame, blood sliding down his chin. Alex was breathing hard. 'Sorry, mate.' He handed Pete some kitchen towel. 'Actually, I'm not sorry. You deserved that, you fuck wit.'

The girl stood up and sidled towards the front door.

'Well, I think maybe I'll be off. Get a night bus or something.'

Neither Pete nor Alex looked at her or tried to stop her. The door clicked shut and she went downstairs slowly and heavily, clearly hoping to be recalled or her departure at least acknowledged.

'Did she have the abortion, then? Did Mand finally get rid of it?'

Alex walked out of the kitchen, pulled the scissor ladder down on to the landing and swung up to the roof, shouldering the hatch aside. It was pretty scuzzy up there, a blackened patch between aerials and eaves, but if you edged round the chimney stacks you could see across great swathes of London. As the Pete-induced adrenalin started to subside, Alex grinned to himself. Insensitive bastard. He had had that coming for weeks.

It was dark but clear, with lit-up tower blocks in the distance, and, unusually, a few tiny stars. Shoving his hand into his pocket, Alex encountered the twisty paper of a spliff and remembered how he'd guessed that morning that he might need it at some stage during the day. Too right. He lit it and sucked greedily in and in as the orange eye flared and crackled in the dark. Tapping off the ash, the end briefly seemed to resemble the eye of a penis but he brushed the thought away and didn't panic. He was slowly starting to feel better. Not all right, exactly, but better. Reality, normality, was flowing back through his veins and reinflating him.

He couldn't see any one person from where he stood, but he knew that London was spread out under him, heaving with people of all shapes and ages doing whatever they were doing. Tina was down below with her sleeping boys, tidying up, reading in bed, possibly, and after tonight could perhaps be counted as a mate. Might he achieve a friendship with a nice woman, without anxiety, sarcasm and the problematic stop-start interface of sexual attraction? How grown-up would that be? He smiled again, tickled by the possibility, alone up on the roof. He hadn't had any decent women friends ever, really; hadn't known how. It might be quite good fun. Mustn't forget about his curry date with her next week.

And that baby – his child, his daughter or son – was it really gone? Hadn't it just been one of his gazillions of sperm that had hung around a bit longer? Why not mourn all the lost possibilities when the condom hadn't broken, or the millions slobbered into a tissue when he'd whacked off in an angry rush, hating Mandy and her pregnancy and wanting all of that business out of his life for good?

He forced himself to try and think calmly how he would have felt tonight if Mandy had refused to go through with the abortion for a second time. He tried to recall the state he'd been in until a few hours ago, the anger and worry and stressed confusion he'd been feeling about it for weeks, sweating in the small hours, fearing that standing order on his bank statement for all time – well, for the next twenty years or however long it was. Christ, did you have to pay for university? Would he want it to be clever?

Slow down. Slow down! The baby, the idea of it, his responsibility to it, his ongoing financial obligation to

Mandy was all gone now, really gone, and tomorrow might be a little bit easier as a result. Perhaps it would work out with Daisy and they could try living together. Maybe they could babysit Jamie and Sam once he knew Tina a bit better. Then she could go out with some mates from work or something and get pissed. Yeah, definitely. He'd suggest it next time he saw her. She'd admitted she might be lonely. He and Pete were categorically growing out of each other too; this evening had been pretty conclusive proof of that, if any were still needed.

It was getting colder and he started to think about going back inside. His heartbeat had slowed down and the stew of his day was no longer slopping against the sides of his head. The baby really had gone. Maybe its tiny soul had become a star or the lights on an aeroplane up above him somewhere. God, that grass had been quite strong. Or perhaps it had splintered into glittering silver fragments suspended against the sky, like the mica bits in Mandy's worktop where he'd left his keys.

Alex flicked his stub far down and out over the roofs, watching the golden sparks arc and spray away from him. This was it, then. Baby, goodbye. Goodbye for ever.

But We Have a History

PAULA SWUNG down the street in the sunshine with a wadge of Saturday papers under her arm, confident that her arse was being clocked by the sexy guy who'd recently started working in Oddbins. She was looking forward to milky coffee, a flick through the magazines and then jumping on Roger if he was still in bed. It's nice to live with someone you fancy, she thought, breaking into a jog to test out her new trainers. She was excited by her haircut, which was quite radical for her, and by getting more responsibility at work. About bloody time. By next summer she should be in charge of all the post-production and in a position to demand a serious pay rise. She'd been at the company for over four years now, and had met Roger in her first week when there'd been a hitch over the effects on one of his ads – shaving cream that danced about. It was pretty naff, as she recalled – certainly hadn't won any awards, but he took it all extremely seriously and that had beguiled her. Paula giggled aloud at the memory and skipped off the kerb. Yup, life was okay.

A few minutes later Roger woke up heavily with a bad feeling either in his head or in his chest, but couldn't work out what was causing it. The duvet hadn't fallen off, the sun was out, and for once Paula had got herself out of bed before him, and it even sounded as though she might be making coffee. The bedroom door was open so he lifted his head to check, dimly remembering sloshing noises from his dreams. Yes, she was in there, hair sleeked down like a seal.

It was a Saturday morning with no work till Monday, so why did he still feel oppressed? It was something to do with last night, he felt sure, irked by the dusty fluff in the grooves of his crappily designed clock-radio. Paula seemed fine. She wouldn't have got up unless she'd been in a good mood so she couldn't have suspected anything. Anyway, there wasn't anything to suspect . . . was there? He'd behaved. More or less. Or stuck, rather, to what he'd promised himself in advance, which was impressive in itself. He had given that blonde sprite a lift home as it was on the way – well, not completely in the wrong direction, at least; allowed himself an extensive goodnight kiss and grope, but no way getting out of the car or phone numbers or any of that nonsense, and it had all gone according to plan. She had nice tits, small and firm, and no bra, he remembered, starting to get a hard-on. That was fine, double fine, in fact, because when he had started apologetically to extricate himself, she had grinned, thanked him for the lift, flicked the light on to check her face and explained she couldn't ask him up because of her boyfriend. What was depressing about that?

The bad feeling was now firmly lodged in his chest, near his heart. Something else must have happened at the party. He needed to comb carefully back through the whole evening to try and identify exactly what it was that was bothering him.

It had been an unexpected situation in which to find himself. Speeding back from Bristol, he had been driven to comment on the horrible train smell that no one else ever appeared to notice or mind and the man opposite him had responded immediately.

'It's the brake fluid, mate.'

'Is that right?'

'What I've been told.'

They had started chatting.

'Do you live in London or are you just visiting? . . . I'm having a party with my flatmate . . . Perhaps you'd like to come?'

Bruno had curly hair, a huge mouth and a chino-clad knee that pressed insistently against Roger's, and as they neared Paddington, light suddenly dawned. Roger smiled nervously and cleared his throat.

'Look, I think I should explain . . .'

The knee was instantly withdrawn.

'No, I'm sorry. Misread the signals with you wanting to talk and everything. Don't look so nervous. It's okay.' Bruno held out his hand and shook Roger's warmly. 'No hard feelings. Promise me?'

Roger shook his head as Bruno swung a sports bag off the luggage rack and headed for the door, calling over his shoulder as he went, 'You will still come to the party?' He scribbled down an address in a designer notebook and ripped out the page.

'It's just off Portobello Road.'

Roger followed him on to the platform, as a reply was called for if only to show that he wasn't homophobic.

'What time?'

'Oh, God, I don't know. Eightish?'

Roger had presented himself at exactly eight fifteen clutching a modest bottle of wine; Paula had refused to accompany him.

'Some man you think was gay who you met on a train? Per*lease*. Would you come to a party I'd been invited to by a dyke at a bus stop?'

Put like that. They had limped half-heartedly through the well-worn routine.

'But we never go to parties.'

'Well, that's because we don't get asked.'

'Why don't we, though?'

'I had loads of friends until I moved in with you.'

'So you always say.'

'You frightened them off.'

'We never take us anywhere.'

This time it ended in giggles, which was less draining, at least, than door-slamming, sulks and silences.

184

'Oh, come on, Paula. Be a sport. I liked the guy. It's an adventure, isn't it?'

'I'm knackered and not in the mood for gut-rot wine in manky plastic cups or shouting at sweaty strangers. Sorry.'

'Well, I am in the mood.'

Roger no longer had a clue whether he was in the mood or not, but having made this much fuss . . . He had scooped up his wallet and left.

Paula spun on her heel, eased an icy Grolsch, bought earlier from the dishy Oddbins guy, out of the fridge and collapsed on to the sofa, confused, suddenly, about how she did actually want to fill her evening. On a whim she punched out her younger sister's mobile number. There were only eighteen months between them, but in most other respects they were light years apart. The phone rang for ages, and when her sister did finally pick up she sounded woozy and startled.

'But you never ring. What's wrong? It's Friday night.'

'Yeah, and I felt like ringing you. What's happening in your life?'

There was a pause and then some sniffing.

'Are you okay?'

More sniffles and a gulp.

'Oi, Jitterbug!'

That finally induced a gaspy snigger from the other end. No one had used that nickname for years. When they were younger, their dad had teased them that a jitterbug was a special jewelled spider and, therefore, the perfect nickname for his daddy-long-legs of a daughter.

There was much nose-blowing going on down the line. To occupy herself, Paula eased off her smart office shoes and frowned at her slug-pale toes squashed into the dark crescent-end of her tights. Dimly she remembered her mother telling her that her younger sister had finally made the break with her husband and moved into this new flat a few weeks ago. Paula had always disliked her brother-in-law's milky freckled skin and obsessive interest in computing. He was shy, dull and lacked presence, but then little Jess had come along and everything had got better for a while. Recently, though, her sister had started seeing some other chap who was quite a bit younger. Apparently this new man and Jess liked each other, but none of the family had met him yet.

Paula dragged out the end of her tights to make her toes look less repulsive.

'How's Jess?'

'She's with her dad.'

'Why were you crying?'

'Because I've just had a fucking abortion. That's why.'

'Christ, I had no idea. You shouldn't be by yourself. Should I come over?'

Roger had taken the car, but she could nip round on his motorbike as this flat her sister was renting was bound to be miles from any known bus or tube route. Luckily she'd only had one beer, as a taxi would cost a fortune.

'Do you need anything?'

'No thanks, I feel crap. Actually . . . maybe some red wine.'

Paula put down the phone and sighed. Still, she wasn't busy, Roger had gone out, and something had obviously made her phone her shambolic younger sister who, unsurprisingly, was in another scrape. Paula, feeling a pleasing surge of bossy protectiveness, checked herself in the mirror – yes, she still looked good – rammed her shoes back on, grabbed her leather jacket and ran off down the stairs.

It was raining as Roger double-checked the number on the house, but no one came to the door for ages. The whole street seemed oddly quiet and he had a sudden twitch of butterflies. The address was clutched nervously in his hand, but when he held it up to try and read it in the dark, the ink ran in the rain. Finally a thin, dark-haired woman opened the door, looking surprised.

'Is this . . . is there a party here?' Roger stammered, thinking, this is absolutely ridiculous. I'm twenty-nine, I work in advertising, I make pitches, rather successfully, as it goes. What's wrong with me?

The woman smiled. She had a gap in her teeth. It was either sexy or odd, Roger couldn't quite decide.

'You're the first to arrive. You must be a friend of Bruno's. Come in.'

Paula's sister opened the door in an outsize lilac T-shirt with a dinosaur duvet wrapped round her lower half. Big-eyed and pale, she eased herself cautiously back down on to the sofa, but once Paula had opened the wine and got some glasses she rallied slightly. Her duvet slipped down on to the floor as she untangled her legs to sit upright and drink more comfortably. Leaning forward to retrieve it, Paula glimpsed the bulky sanitary pad in a quick flash of goose-pimpled thighs and black lacy briefs. Poor cow. Concern and then irritation rippled under Paula's skin in waves. Her kid sister was still such a baby, and her life seemed repeatedly to skid off course. Paula had always made a point of having her jobs, lovers and emotions tidily taped down and labelled, whereas her incontinent sister by contrast generated pools of mess around herself and then flailed about in them squawking.

Gently, Paula tidied snotty tissues and crumpled magazines off the sofa.

'So . . . where's your boyfriend, then? Does he know?'

Her sister's shoulders started to shake and she shook her head but didn't reply.

'What? Look, I don't mean to get at you.'

Her sister dipped a finger in the wine and started to paint the outside of the glass with it.

'He took me to, you know, the clinic thingy, but then he left.'

It was unlikely that Paula would ever need an abortion, but if she ever did, she thought to herself, idly worrying about her sister's split ends, you could be absolutely sure that Roger would flipping well be dancing attendance with lashings of hot-water bottles and lemon barley water. Gently, Paula traced round the delicate wings of her sister's shoulderblades, trying to shake the feeling that they were both on stage.

'Is there anything I can do? Shall I ring him for you? He should know if you're feeling lousy, shouldn't he?'

Mandy took a long, shuddery breath, a legacy of her crying jag earlier.

'We split up. He didn't want to be with me any more. And . . . and Jess really liked him. And so did I. And that's why I feel crap. Not because of the fucking abortion. It wasn't even his baby, it was Vaughan's. But I thought Alex and I'd get back together again. I really did. He likes kids.'

Trying to process all of this, Paula took a deep breath and patted her sister's knee through the duvet.

'Well, it was nice of Alex to take you then, wasn't it? When you'd split up and it wasn't even his baby.'

Mandy put her wine down, hunched up her knees and banged her head down on them.

'Yeah, but he thought it was his. It seemed easier that way. I don't want to be with Vaughan any more. I really don't. I just did it once, by mistake. I got a bit pissed and we'd played Star Wars Monopoly with Jess, and I just sort of gave in. I don't know why. I felt crap afterwards. I knew it was a mistake. Alex was very careful and always used a condom so I told him it must have broken, and maybe it had, but I don't think so. I'm pretty sure the baby was Vaughan's.'

What in God's name had she been playing at? Had Mand been planning to have Vaughan's baby and pretend it was Alex's, or what, exactly? Maybe she hadn't even thought it through that far. What a lash-up. Paula was reeling, but even she realised it wasn't quite the moment to lay into her sister. For the moment, at least, she decided simply to side-step the whole sorry mess.

'Look, hon, you've had a helluva day and you must be knackered. I think you should get into bed properly.'

Surprisingly, Mandy didn't argue. Paula tipped the end of the bottle into her sister's glass, occasioning a sad little toasting gesture.

'Thanks for coming round. But I haven't asked anything about you.'

Paula shook her head. 'Don't worry about it. It's fine. Just get yourself into bed and keep warm. Give Jess my love.'

Zipping up her luscious jacket rather too emphatically, she tried to give her sister a kiss, but somehow they ended up crashing heads and then kissed each other on the mouth by mistake.

'Chin up, Jitterbug. I'll call you.'

*

The galley kitchen was crammed with food in various states of undress which Bruno was attempting to sort out. Rosa, Bruno's flat mate and the woman who had opened the door, sat Roger down and got him a beer. As she pottered about, he started to relax and make suggestions about the music and lighting, and she even asked his advice on her dress. Roger didn't want to hurt her feelings, but had warmed to her to such a degree by then that he cautiously ventured a view that the overall effect was a little unrelieved. Did she have any jewellery? She thanked him and razzed herself up with lashings of sparkly accessories. She was probably about forty, and Roger really liked her. They went on talking.

As Bruno buzzed about taking wet coats, the room started to fill up. Rosa knew a lot about photography and design, and after a few beers and their longish conversation, Roger started to feel warmly complacent about the evening overall. Bruno was a good host and checked every half-hour or so that Roger had someone to talk to and a fullish glass. Some of the guests had jobs and some didn't, but they all appeared intrigued by advertising and posters and campaigns. Roger dressed his job down a bit and slid it slightly nearer the creative department than it actually was. He neglected to mention Paula, but she could have come and hadn't wanted to, so that seemed like a fair cop. He chatted for a while to a television producer who was worried about getting back to her toddler, and then danced with Rosa. She seemed to know most of the guests and was affectionate and relaxed with everyone there, resting on a shoulder to light her cigarette or easing someone's hips aside to slide through the crowd.

It got late. It had been a good party, had shaken down well and people had circulated, but now it was starting to fragment and lose momentum. Roger realised that social fatigue had crept up on him and he was starting to feel fuzzy. He and a small blonde had been giving each other all-in-good-time looks for most of the evening. As he checked his watch and gathered himself up to leave, she signalled that she was coming too, and slung on a raincoat that momentarily put him off. Roger found Bruno, and said goodbye and thank you he'd really enjoyed it, which he had. He felt a twinge about Rosa but couldn't instantly locate her, so fought his way down the passage to the door.

It was raining lightly and he put his arm protectively round the blonde girl's shoulders. As they walked down the path there was a flurry at the front door. Rosa was standing there; the heel had snapped off one of her shoes, and she bent over to investigate it, exposing black lace. Roger stared at her, alarmed, as she straightened up. She was almost crying as she looked over at the blonde girl in the ugly raincoat, bewildered. Her eyes seemed to be signalling to Roger in amongst the hurt, 'But we had a history . . . I thought we were friends . . . I don't understand . . .' In his mind he went back up the path, stroked the hair out of her face, took her back inside and reassured her. 'You're right. There's been a brief confusion, but it's all fine now.' But the blonde was out of the gate and looking back impatiently at Roger. He panicked, strode over to her and scooped her off round the corner, leaving Rosa horribly exposed on the doorstep, holding her broken shoe. That's why he felt bad, and at last there was some relief in identifying the sore bit and probing it.

Pouring out the coffee and feeling momentarily queasy about her younger sister, Paula flicked a short blonde hair off the lapel of Roger's jacket. It was the one he'd worn yesterday evening and then dumped in a heap on the kitchen table. Typical! She'd tease him about blondes after she'd seduced him, maybe, but she wasn't remotely worried. Roger was lucky to have her. She didn't need to police him. Satisfied, Paula reckoned she had definitely made the right call by opting out of a dodgy-sounding party and then disrupting a rare evening in alone to go off and comfort shambolic Mand. Reviewing her own life, everything, by contrast, did seem in spectacularly good order; her buoyant mood of earlier justified. She remembered sprawling across the whole bed last night so that Roger would have to move her to find a space. She always enjoyed that – his bundling her over very gently, unsure how deeply asleep she was. He had come in lateish but not worryingly so, kissed her, murmured at her, and although it was good to have him back beside her, she had been too tired to wake up properly or reply to him. Now, though, after a good night's sleep . . .

Roger was toying with getting up when Paula brought him in some coffee, shook her wet hair and started investigating him under the duvet. Shame about her haircut as it felt a bit like making love to a boy. Not one of his fantasies, as it went. Still, it would grow soon enough, and she did have a great body.

'Did you miss me? Did you pull?'

She paused briefly to peel off her knickers and then put his cock in her mouth as Roger determinedly clung on to his thought process. It had taken him long enough to recall everything and he wasn't quite ready to return to the present yet. He hadn't really fancied Rosa at any stage, but he'd liked her immensely, enjoyed her company and been charmed by Bruno's warmth and generosity. They were unusually cool, in fact. Both of them. What on earth had got into him? To have failed to say goodbye to Rosa was unforgivable and he knew it. How shameful. Shit. His lust for horrible raincoat had won out with absolutely no struggle. They'd even had a quick smooch in the street, he remembered, and then sniggered about Rosa as they'd got into his car, dismissing her as drunk and elderly. That was really tacky. That's why he felt so lousy about the whole thing.

Paula slithered back up the bed.

'Sorry. Can't give you a blow job when your cock's that big. It hurts my jaw. Seriously.' Then she was astride him, hands on his shoulders rocking harder and harder and laughing.

'So tell me about the blonde girl you picked up last night.'

'What blonde girl?'

Fuck.

Property of . . .

AGENTS USUALLY went out in pairs, but as the client was an elderly female librarian, Lindy volunteered to meet her at the property alone. She was keen to make a good impression as it was only her second week with Alan Sandler Estates. The day was glaringly hot, and, failing to find a parking spot with even a wisp of shade, Lindy decided to wait up in the flat for her prospective tenant. She was in excellent time and identified it easily enough, a ropey conversion just off the main road. As her stomach had ground away insistently at her during the drive, she had ripped back the egg-smeared cellophane on her sandwich while she was waiting, but had then changed her mind. She was too new still to risk being interrupted by the client mid-scoff with a greasy mouth and crumbs cascading down her lilac regulation blouse.

Poking about to fill the time, Lindy tried to picture someone living here until a few days ago, ironing or putting away the shopping. She spotted a child's pink teddy-bear hairclip in the bathroom and a stub of amber washing-up liquid on the kitchen window sill, but that seemed to be all. Bored now, as well as ravenous, Lindy sat down with a whoomph on the sofa, which was lower and lighter than she had anticipated and skidded off sideways under her. Jumping up, she was dutifully shoving it back into near perfect alignment with the wall when one of the castors encountered some kind of doughy resistance and stuck fast. Lindy leant forward, her waistband biting into her stomach, and retrieved a bright candy-striped notebook from where the sofa had scrunched it up against the wainscoting.

Carefully smoothing out the buckled-up pages, she realised that she had picked up someone's diary. The entries made at daily intervals were of wildly differing lengths, but had all been written with the same blobby black biro. Lindy riffled through the pages, clocking entries at random, before lowering herself cautiously back down on to the sofa. The sun was belting in on her now, and although her face was fiery both from the effort of retrieving the notebook and from reading something that was clearly private, she couldn't bear to stop and open a window. She was utterly engrossed when the doorbell finally rang and she realised that she was obliged to stop reading and go downstairs to greet her client.

'Anthea Blackburn, like the place.' Or the DJ, thought Lindy bleakly, tracing round a wheatsheaf motif on the grimy beige toaster. She knew that she should be gentling Anthea along, humouring her to secure the let, but she couldn't bear to prolong the encounter.

'What? Sorry?'

Anthea was slightly concerned about the area. Did Lindy have any experience of this stretch of the main road? There seemed to be a few pubs and take-aways, didn't there? Might it be quite noisy in the evenings? Were there young children in the flats on either side? Would it be possible to find out?

Lindy was keen to have a baby herself, but Robert was insisting that they hang on until they had a bit more money, somewhere with a garden. Half conscious of Anthea twittering on, Lindy felt superstitious that the fate of any baby she might or might not conceive in the future was somehow linked with the story in the crumpled notebook. You had to stamp on that kind of nonsense, though, as soon as it occurred to you. Lindy knew that. Otherwise your whole life could become dominated by the moment that traffic lights changed, or the number of cracks between paving stones when you were pretending not to care where you were putting your feet.

As Anthea finally faffed her way back down the path, promising repeatedly to make a decision in the next couple of days, Lindy glanced openly at her watch. She had already been away longer than she had intended. Double-locking the flimsy front door, she zipped up her shoulder bag with the notebook still in there, lying alien atop the mulch of old tissues and make-up. She'd never stolen anything before in her life. Was this stealing? No, it was tidying up. In which case should she chuck it in a dustbin or take it back to the office to be returned to the owner? It was only a cheap notebook, though, and the previous tenant, or her friend or sister, had had nearly a week to reclaim it if they had wanted to, if it had mattered.

As Lindy marched back through the office towards her desk, her dangling shoulder bag felt radioactive, a glowing rectangle pulsing out signals to alert her bored associates.

'Will Anthea take it?'

'Um, she's not sure, yet,' Lindy heard herself mumble dully, realising that she simply couldn't bear to wait another instant before setting off for the privacy of the loo. Swerving in the direction of the ladies, she felt her hand clamp itself tightly over the bag as if the diary might try and climb out by itself en route.

'Time of the month,' she mouthed nervously at a female colleague when she emerged twenty minutes later, flushed and flustered. Hunched in the tiny cubicle she'd been riveted by every beat of the story, carefully reading through the first third in the order that it had been written, this time, rather than dotting back and forth. She realised that she wanted to read the rest with actual names in mind. The writer's daughter's name began with a J unless the letters were a code rather than initials which seemed unlikely.

Jane? Jemima? Jade, maybe, and V was an usual initial for a man. Victor was all Lindy could come up with, unless it was a Vikram or a Veejay. V was the dumped husband who worked with computers. The younger lover could be Andrew, perhaps, or Anthony, but Lindy didn't know what he did yet.

She looked up nervously from her screen and coughed.

'Who had that flat on the Highway last?'

A woman over by the coffee machine did mug-miming gestures to Lindy, who shook her head distractedly. A few seconds later Sammy, shifty, carroty, and, in office speak, a bit of a chancer, looked up.

'Broad named Mandy and her daughter. Why?'

'Just wondered.' Lindy's heart was thumping. 'Anthea seemed a bit worried about the area. Maybe it would reassure her to know the previous tenants were a woman and her daughter.'

'Whatever.' Sammy had almost lost interest. 'Mandy was a stunner. All over the place, but a real stunner.'

'Is she still on our books, then?'

'Nah. Said she was moving in with her boyfriend. Saw him when they dropped off the keys. A lot older than her.' Sammy winked. 'Well, good luck to her, eh? When she gets bored of him, I'll be waiting!' He tapped his chunky rings against the desk, indicating that the subject was now closed, before hopscotching over to the filing cabinet.

Lindy was sure A was younger than Mandy. Would she say boyfriend, though, if it was her ex-husband? Maybe this man was someone new? It was tantalising having different bits of the puzzle in her possession now, but not quite enough information to complete the picture.

All through supper that evening, Lindy's mind was working overtime. Fortunately Robert was so incensed by his day and an uptight female supervisor who had been picking on him that he didn't notice Lindy's unconvincing responses. She practised her little spiel in her head, her back turned to him as she washed up, before clattering dishes on to the draining board and saying 'Bother' a bit too loudly. Then she rifled ostentatiously through her bag and upended it. 'Nope, it's not there.' Robert, deep in a television documentary about injured race horses, failed to respond, but Lindy ploughed on anyway.

'I think I've left the key I need for my viewing tomorrow in the office. I'd better go and check.'

Reluctantly, Robert dragged his eyes away from a close-up of damaged cartilage. 'Can't you get it tomorrow?'

Lindy shook her head and sighed. 'Nope, there'll be too much traffic. I'd best pop back and get it now. I really don't want to be late for my morning appointment.'

The purple façade of Alan Sandler Estates was eerie at this time of night and, looking up at it, Lindy almost lost her nerve. It seemed pathetic to give up now, though, so she scuttled across to the main doors, looking nervously over her shoulder and digging out her office keys. Once she was safely inside, she flicked on a couple of anglepoises on desks as she passed, hoping that they would be less noticeable from the street than a wash of ceiling lights. If anyone caught her, she would just have to improvise. Anyway, she wasn't doing anything wrong, just snooping at a time when she wouldn't have to explain to anyone what she was after.

It involved her in a bit of detective work, cross-referencing Sammy's appointments' diary with the property files, but pretty soon she had Mandy's tenancy form and, as she'd hoped, a mobile number. She copied it carefully into her own diary with the word diary next to it, and then, as the adrenalin that had got her to this next stage slowly subsided, her nerves returned and she hurtled back out again, turning off the lights and relocking the doors in fumbling haste.

Parking a couple of streets away from her own flat, she checked that the car doors were locked and opened Mandy's dairy, reading a bit more by the tiny bulb in the glove compartment, as she was worried that the overhead light might make her too con-spicuous. She got to the second abortion visit, which, this time, as Lindy now knew, having flicked ahead earlier, Mandy saw through. Then she stopped reading and drove back to her own flat. When she'd parked for a second time she put her hand flat across her stomach and tried to imagine the before and after, the little imagined flutterings followed by the pains and seeping loss.

Robert hadn't moved from the sofa, but glanced up as she came in.

'Everything all right?'

'Fine,' said Lindy, more defensively than she had intended.

'Look as though you've been crying.'

But Robert wasn't really bothered. He turned back to the screen for the football results as Lindy ducked back to check her face in the hall mirror. Her mascara was smudged and, to her surprise, her cheeks were glistening. She burrowed in her jacket pocket for a tissue and scrubbed at her eyes. 'Grit,' she muttered. 'Something in my eye,' before going back into their living area and twitching the kettle switch out of nerves as she passed.

'Cup of tea, love?'

Robert held up a beer can in response without turning his head.

Lindy had been crying for the baby but hadn't realised it. How absurd. She must get a grip. Maybe Mandy had a different mobile number now and that would be that. Maybe her older lover had given her a new phone as a moving-in present, a flash one that took pictures and sent emails. This would really be her only shot, as Sammy would think he was working with a nutter or stalker if she asked him for any more information.

The following day, Lindy dialled the number during her lunch break from a bench in a dusty little park. Her chest felt tight. The mobile the other end rang at length and was eventually answered. Having established that it was Mandy on the other end, Lindy hummed and haa-ed and explained about the diary. Mandy had wondered where it had got to but didn't sound overly concerned. Panicking that this phone call might suddenly end, Lindy asked where Mandy lived and said she could easily drop it off the next day as she had a house to check out in that area.

'Yeah, that'd be great, thanks. I should be around until lunchtime.'

The following morning, once Robert had set off, Lindy called in to work with flu. Sometimes they left together, and Lindy loved tripping out of the front door with her husband, both of them showered and smartly dressed for work. It made her feel as though she was in a story or a Eurostar promotion as half of a busy and well organised couple, and quite often she gave him a lift to the tube to prolong that sensation. Fortunately today, though, he had a big meeting to prepare for and was keen to get off before she was ready.

A bit later, driving through Mandy's wealthy suburb, squinting at the A to Z open on the seat beside her, Lindy did wonder briefly what on earth she was doing. She seemed to have generated a momentum around herself that had nothing to do with her usual behaviour and responses.

The house, when she finally found it, was built from ugly mustard brick in a broad avenue of similar-sized variants, all kitted out with automatic gates and carriage lamps. Mandy opened the door wearing low-slung jeans and a sparkly Barbie T-shirt which Lindy couldn't help staring at. Mandy noticed and smiled at her.

'My boyfriend gave it to me for Jessie – that's my daughter – but I thought it was a bit too sexy for her. I don't like all that stuff, make-up and boob tubes for little girls. Do you know what I mean?'

Lindy smiled and nodded before quickly shaking her head. 'Yes. I mean, no. You're right.' Her mind was whirling as she tried to process the information. J was for Jessie, then. She would never have guessed that, and Mandy wasn't married to this new guy yet if she called him her boyfriend. Sammy had been right, though. Mandy was a real stunner, with dirty blonde hair, an absurdly good figure and unnaturally white, slightly wonky front teeth.

'Look, do you want a coffee or are you in a rush?'

In a bit of a daze, Lindy followed the long denim legs back down the hall into the elegant kitchen, and while Mandy was blasting water into a designer kettle, fished the diary out of her bag and laid it on the table.

Mandy moved it on to the dresser as she lifted down some pretty mugs.

'Better not leave it lying around. Some of it's a bit personal, if you know what I mean, but I do fancy looking through it again. You forget things . . . Have you got any kids?'

Lindy, startled, knocked her mouth against the mug, slopping coffee on to the shiny tabletop. Did Mandy know she'd read it? Expect her to have read it? Was it a trick question? It seemed unlikely as she appeared utterly without guile. She was clearly proud of her shiny utensils and large smart garden, though. 'Nice here, innit?' she said when Lindy seemed unable to answer the kids question one way or another.

'It's lovely,' replied Lindy, jerking herself back into the conversation. 'No, we haven't got any children, but I'd like some soon, I think.'

Mandy grinned. 'I love my Jessie to bits, of course I do, but you're more tied than you would be without. Dancing, clubbing, drinking and that with your mates – you don't want to jack it all in just 'cos you've got a kid, but it does make it harder.'

Her words, her figure, her pretty heart-shaped face spun round in Lindy's head as she drove back. She tried to think when she and Robert had last gone out. They weren't tied down but they behaved as though they were, and they hadn't even got any children yet. They were inhibited by routine, she supposed, and lack of money and anxiety when the interest rates went up, and seeing Robert's mum most weekends as she didn't have anyone else. Lindy had never skived before in her life, so daringly she decided she'd better make the most of today and do something nice. Perhaps she could drive down to the South Bank and window-shop at Gabriel's Wharf or just potter along by the river for a bit. Tomorrow, refreshed and motivated, she'd go back to work and be decisive and professional and go for that bonus. And when she'd got the bonus, she'd force Robert to think seriously about having 'kids'. The word in her head was said with Mandy's accent and smile.

Lindy wasn't given to flights of fancy, but it seemed to her suddenly that her life was like a neatly wrapped brown paper parcel. She knew its shape and what it was likely to contain. She and Robert would stay together and she would go on doing her job and he his and eventually they might be able to move into something a little further out with a garden for those kids. Lindy giggled. They'd multiplied during the journey. She parked in a pay-and-display gap and nipped into M&S to select a treatish picnic lunch for herself, wondering what Mandy's life was like by contrast – an unravelling cracker, perhaps, with much more colour and confusion, a live-for-the-day motto, a pink paper hat and the novelty item, a plastic baby-doll keyring.

Lindy ended up sitting on the jetty down by the Oxo Tower, her lunch arranged neatly beside her, delighting in the sunshine bouncing off the water. After the last somewhat hectic twenty-four hours, Mandy had been laid to rest and she and Lindy would continue their separate lives unlinked. Mandy was unlikely to give Lindy another moment's thought, Lindy realised with a small shock, but she, Lindy, would refer to Mandy from time to time whenever she felt she was getting too stuck in the mud, too predictable. Mandy could be a secret sign to her, a reminder to live a little more dangerously. She looked out across the little stretch of scuzzy beach. Perhaps she should start to step up the pressure on Robert for babies.

After about twenty minutes, a well-built man wandered past, swigging mineral water. The sun was administering real punch, and as he eased himself down on to the planks, he wriggled his shoulders with pleasure. Catching Lindy looking over at him, he grinned.

'Isn't it great down here today?'

She smiled back and nodded enthusiastically. After her rather intense dialogue with herself, she felt like some company and as he was clearly too nice to presume, she cast around for something neutral to add. A black rubbish barge was slipping past them in the middle of the river and she pointed at it.

'My great-grandfather was a lighter-man. Don't imagine the actual boats have changed much.'

The man smiled again. 'Funny to imagine what the

actual rubbish consisted of in those days. Nothing synthetic, I don't suppose. Newspapers, empty tins and vegetable peelings. Unless, of course, you had a compost heap.'

They started to chat easily and comfortably about how string and buttons were carefully kept then, whereas now that kind of hoarding was thought a bit odd. Lindy remembered her mum's little walnut button box that she had been allowed to pay with as a treat whenever she was sick. She told the man that although she hadn't thought about it for years and years, she could still describe almost every button that had been in the box: pretty green glass stars, small white shirt buttons, and large tweedy monsters with loops on the back instead of holes.

'Where is it now?'

Lindy didn't know. Strangely, she felt she might cry. Lost buttons and babies. What was happening to her? Then she observed quite openly, almost without knowing what she was saying, 'I can't imagine having this conversation with my husband.'

The man looked away across the water. 'That's often the way, though, isn't it? Sometimes it seems so much easier to talk when you haven't got a history.'

Lindy, concerned that she had been disloyal to Robert, was happy with his response, although wistful that this easy state of no history between her and this man by definition couldn't last beyond a first encounter.

They sat on in silence, gently licked by the dipping sun, set apart somehow from their usual routines. Would they get up in a minute and go their different ways? Anything else would seem inappropriate. As Lindy wondered, the man solved it for her by scribbling his name and number on a scrap of picnic bag.

'Look, I know you're married, but . . . if you're ever not, or feel like another picnic, here's my number. I'm divorced. Just so you know.'

Lindy took it but didn't look up at him. She really, really wanted to know what had gone wrong, and finally the urge to discover won out over her habitual restraint.

'Why?'

'Simple, really. She didn't want kids and I did.'

Lindy felt a rush of happiness and pleasure, but didn't know how to express it. It suddenly seemed immensely important to her to behave decently and properly to everyone around her. Her happiness would depend on getting the minute-by-minute detail of things right from now on as well as the big future direction of her funny little life.

'What is it that you do?' she asked, stalling and picking at a splinter before tidying together the remains of her food.

The man looked down at her. 'I'm a cop, which you might find off-putting. A pretty junior one, actually, but still a policeman,' and he was gone, turning back once, decisively, to wave at her from the bank.

Lindy knew she had to get up and go home and go in to work tomorrow and all of that. Just for a few minutes, though, she thought she'd allow herself to contemplate the weird, tranquil bubble she found herself encased in, now, in the early afternoon on the river, at the end of her mad treasure-hunt trail. She could almost feel the experience of today brushing against her cheeks. The real her and the unreal her or the old her and the new her – which was it to be? It all spun round her future, or not, with Robert. Dissatisfactions or changing needs usually stacked up slowly, over months, but maybe occasionally you should take a big leap. Perhaps she'd been quietly fizzing away without knowing, and intersecting with Mandy's mad zig-zags like this was a symptom of her need for a change. It could equally easily have been precipitated by something else, a serious row with Robert, a promotion, a cervical-cancer scare.

The sun was behind a cloud now and Lindy wished that she'd brought her jacket with her from the car. She headed back along the bank, celebrating the fact of Mandy in her low-slung jeans and sparkly T-shirt like a special saint or figurehead. Lindy hoped fervently that she'd have the courage to make the right choices for herself for her own future, whatever in the end that turned out to be.

Departure

Tom had quietly worshipped Jeanette since university and she'd never quite let him slip out of her orbit. He wasn't officially on her guest-list for parties, but would somehow get phoned at the last minute and always seemed free to come – quiet, dependable and never without a bottle of wine. Tom had straight brown hair, wore glasses and wasn't in any way conventionally handsome, but the openness of his face, his obvious decency, did make him attractive. Jeanette recognised that, even if she rued the fact that his image wasn't really up there or racy enough to enhance her own persona. None of her friends could understand why she'd married him, but Jeanette knew exactly. It was about time she had a baby.

Although thirty-seven wasn't that old, she had always been competitive and realised that, if she enjoyed the experience, she might decide to have three or four – outdo some of her friends who were already on the case. Tom was decent, hardworking and easy to control; not electrifying as attributes, perhaps, but spectacularly absent from her last few lovers. In addition he would be faithful to her, support her and be polite to her parents. If she got bored, she thought that perhaps she could discreetly revisit some of her previous lovers. After all, it was hard to know in advance what being married would feel like, but only sleeping with one man for the rest of her life didn't appeal to her. Well, not at this stage. She was strong, fit, good at sex, and did feel that more than one chap should get the benefit. If, when she was older and a mother things seemed different, then that would be fine as well. Tom was good insurance and she was just being sensible keeping her options open by getting married.

Tom, in turn, couldn't quite get over the fact that Jeanette had suggested they get married and then almost immediately happily become pregnant. He was besotted with his small son and hoped that fairly soon they might have another child, move out of London and so on. He didn't care to rush Jeanette away from her metropolitan pleasures, though, before she was ready, and was supremely sensitive to what she might just tolerate and what she absolutely would not. For instance, she was avid about films, and that hadn't diminished with the baby's arrival. Jeanette liked to go the moment that the movie, as she called it, had opened in order to impress her acquaintance with her energy and savvy, up-to-date views, particularly having just given birth.

'Gosh, Jeanette, have you seen that already?'

'You are amazing.'

'I don't know how you do it.'

And so on.

Tom was more than happy to babysit Seamus; an odd name, but it had been pushed for by Jeanette and Tom hadn't disliked it enough to argue.

They had piecemeal childcare as Tom, a GP, was hired by a North London practice, and had no afternoon or evening surgery on Thursdays, while Jeanette worked part time for a company that organised events. She was only paid for three days, although she did seem to be doing more and more. Even though their childminder welcomed extra money, the lack of routine and last-minute changes troubled Tom. He never knew when he came home from work where Jeanette or the baby might have ended up. Sometimes she went away for the night. There might, for example, be a dinner-dance in Manchester for the area managers of mobile phone sales people and Jeanette's company would be contracted to realise the event, sorting out the venue, the catering and identifying some wacky theme or other. Jeanette's part, aside from attending endless brainstorming sessions, at which, she prided herself, she was rather creative, would be to babysit the minor celebrity whom her company had booked for added fizz.

Tom was never quite sure how it all worked, and Jeanette, while clearly enjoying the actual jaunts, was disparaging about the people she was obliged to mix with. They both knew there was something seedy and desperate about the events themselves. Jeanette would name-drop to friends while simultaneously back-pedalling about the overall tackiness of the functions she had helped to organise. Tom didn't discuss it with her much; was just happy to have her back, snide and tired. Anyway, his evenings alone with Seamus were good fun. They'd eat supper together and maybe have a water-fight as it was easier to indulge in the high-voltage horseplay that Seamus really loved when Jeanette wasn't around.

The more time Tom spent with his son, the happier they both were. He got double dollops of pleasure, as he saw it, from being a doctor-father watching his son scramble up and over the different developmental hurdles. That's great, he'd think with a warm glow, followed by, yes, gosh, he's fifteen months old, so he should be achieving that. Seamus wasn't particularly gifted, nor was he unusually slow. He just was. He had Jeanette's big china-blue eyes and her determined chin. Tom loved the fact that the two additional bits of his family were so clearly part of each other, obviously physically interlinked. It made him feel secure and he felt that he gained extra lustre by his connection with them both.

Tom and Seamus used to frequent the café at the bottom of their road until its creepy proprietor topped himself. Then new owners, hairy sweaty hippies, changed the menu. The watery tea and slabs of dry cake that they served up were not to Tom's taste, so on his Thursday afternoons with Seamus, when the weather got warmer, they gravitated to Queen's Park instead. It was a pleasant push away, and they both liked the miniature zoo and the old fashioned bandstand. While Seamus pottered about with his bucket and spade in the vast circular sandpit, Tom read his periodicals. He felt slightly bad about not giving his son one hundred per cent of his attention during their time together, but Seamus was happy enough and Tom needed to get on top of the new drug trials and so on. Once the baby was in bed and Jeanette and he had eaten and got through a bottle of wine, it was hard to get focused on new treatments for asthma or depression. He'd always been conscientious, though, and was concerned not to get slipshod and start letting his patients down just because he had a young child.

The sun shone and Tom, even as he wrestled with dense medical detail, was attuned to his son's wants, aware of Seamus's scarlet dungarees like a minute sunspot on the edge of his peripheral vision. Becoming conscious of some kind of kerfuffle, he looked up. A pretty toddler of about Seamus's age with clouds of dark hair had grabbed his son's spade while he was in mid-bucket-fill. Tom smiled to himself, gave his glasses an anxious shove on his nose and stood up to arbitrate. Before he'd opened his mouth, the little girl took a swing at Seamus's head with the spade and missed him entirely, but was so incensed by her own ineptitude that she then strode forward and shoved him hard in the chest. Startled off balance, the little boy lurched, cracking the bridge of his nose on the metal lip of the slide, and blood started splashing down on to the sand. Tom flew to his side, scooped him up and held him tight, getting a purchase for his own broad back against a stationary roundabout. Seamus was bellowing now in outrage and pain, tears and snot mixing with the blood as Tom held him and soothed him, waiting for him to calm down. 'Ssshhhh. There, sweetheart, brave boy, naughty slide. You went bang, didn't you? Bang!' This at least elicited the tiniest whimper of a possible snigger from against Tom's shoulder, and, somewhat heartened, he set the little boy down and gently investigated the wound.

For the last few seconds Tom had been conscious of a woman squatting a few feet away, and as his adrenalin subsided she swam into focus. She seemed delicate, but at the same time more vivid than the other more run-of-the-mill parents and carers. Maybe it was down to the bright scarf she was wearing. Tom searched for the adjective he wanted, unaccustomed to thinking in this way. The woman was exotic, that was it, and when she spoke to him a moment later it turned out she was American as well.

'Is your little guy okay? Is there anything I can do?'

'I think he's fine,' replied Tom cautiously. 'It's nice of you to offer.'

'Oh, it's the least I can do. My daughter was the one who hurt him.'

'I don't think she meant to,' rejoined Tom politely.

The woman looked him straight in the face. 'I'm afraid she did. Recently she's become a total toy Nazi and I don't know what to do about it.'

How odd, thought Tom, to be drawn to someone whose child had caused your own to be hurt. He found her clear-eyed frankness about her own child appealing, and, looking at her, could see where her daughter got her charm from. The woman held out her hand, enquiring and concerned, head cocked sideways. She seemed to him like a pretty little thrush or butterfly who'd landed unexpectedly on his foot.

'Howdy, I'm Rose. Are you sure he's okay?'

Tom shook her hand and smiled. 'Yes, I'm absolutely sure.'

Rose raised her eyebrows quizzically.

'I'm a doctor.'

'Are you kidding me?'

Tom shook his head. There was a pause. Rose thoughtfully moved Seamus's pushchair a bit closer while Tom had been comforting his son, and she'd also rescued his medical journal, which had been blowing off towards the swings. Taking it out now from where she had stuffed it in the top of her little leather rucksack, she looked at it wryly.

'I guess you're for real. Nobody would read this stuff

for pleasure, would they? Unless, of course, they were a pervert.'

They both started to laugh.

'I'm Tom and this is Seamus. He's eighteen months.'

'Oh, so's Esme.'

'Esme? That's a pretty name.' Exotic he thought privately, smiling inside.

'It's a Salinger story. You know, "For Esme with Love and Squalor".'

Tom shook his head confused.

'*The Catcher in the Rye* guy. It's a great collection. You should read it, specially if you like kids.'

Tom was intrigued. No one had suggested he read a story before, ever! He'd done sciences since his mid-teens, and before that, God, before that, well, boys' adventure books, he supposed. Willard Price? He couldn't really remember, but perhaps wouldn't bring that up now as the last fiction that he'd encountered twenty-odd years ago, even though, as the author was American, she might have come across him. There was no good reason, though, why he couldn't read a story, enjoy it even. How shocking that it was such a shocking thought.

Rose and he chattered away easily enough, he sitting and she squatting on the edge of the sandpit area. They kept a wary eye on both children, with Rose occasionally leaping up to expostulate with Esme. Rose was a theatre designer, but hadn't worked since she'd had Esme as she couldn't travel around the country now very easily and do twenty-four hour get-ins and all of that stuff. Her partner worked long hours, she said, in local government and she, Rose, was happy to keep house for a bit and hang out with her daughter.

'Might as well enjoy her, monster that she is. I'm nearly forty-six and not about to have another one, sadly. She was a last-chance-and-then-some baby. Perhaps that's why she behaves so badly on occasion. She senses that for me she's really, really special and can get away with major misdemeanours'

'I think most kids are special to their parents,' observed Tom mildly. He mentally reviewed some of the grimmer cases of neglect and abuse he'd had to deal with recently, but decided against embarking on all of that just now. It seemed as unhelpful to this delicate little encounter as his dated lion and tiger boys' adventure stories would have been.

Rose smiled. 'Yeah, I know. I probably over-scrutinise her. Poor pumpkin.'

Tom realised he liked her diction: misdemeanour, scrutinise. His world felt bigger and more alive in her presence. He never noticed colours or shapes in the usual run of things, but was still enormously struck by Rose's swaggering scarf. It was scarlet and russet and golden and crimson and lit up her cheeks. She fiddled absent-mindedly with the fringe as she spoke. Yes, he thought. I'm going to. Why not?

'I really like your scarf.'

'Good,' she said. 'It was shockingly expensive. Linen and flax, don't you know?' Now she was sending herself up.

They started sorting out the joint paraphernalia of changing bags and juice beakers and got up to go. Flax, he thought, patting sand off Seamus's feet. Another satisfying click of a word. It sounded almost medieval.

'The flax fields in Suffolk,' he told her, 'where I grew up are a lovely misty blue and they look beautiful when the poppies come out.'

'That's cool,' she said. 'I don't think I even knew that flax flowers were blue. I loathe watercolours on the whole, such a wimpy medium, but Nolde did blazing watercolours of poppies. They really are shouts of painting. All those Germans in the thirties used such ferociously intense colours. Do you know the Blue Rider school?'

Tom shook his head, alarmed by the galloping off of his modest flax moment into such alien territory. Books he could maybe buy and read, but sourcing watercolours from the last century seemed more ambitious.

'Well, you should,' she said emphatically, twisting the tone into something playfully intimate with her insistence. 'Those pictures are medicine, and that's your thing, isn't it?'

Grinning at him, she gestured at his periodical, now buried under wipes and clean nappies in Seamus's changing bag. By this time they had reached one of the corner gates to the park and were forking off back to their separate lives.

A couple of Thursdays later as Tom left the park, Rose tore after him. She was shouting his name with an exhilarated Esme rattling along in front of her, hair streaming and pushchair wheels jouncing off the path.

'Jeez, I really hoped I'd see you. You weren't here last week?'

Tom was thrilled if startled by the vigour of her approach.

'Seamus had a bug so we had to stay indoors.'

Rose yanked a beaten-up old paperback out of her rucksack.

'This is the book I was telling you about. I don't want it back. It's a present. The least I could do after my daughter's viciousness. Um. There's three stories with kids, here, see?' She'd drawn tiny red stars by them in the index. 'Well, they're my favourites. Hope you like them!'

And she was gone, clattering off with her second-hand buggy before Tom, charmed by the unexpected encounter, could muster the words to thank her.

They bumped into each other most Thursdays after that. Rose extolled the joys of the world or aired her pet dislikes, while Tom pottered along in her mental wake, confused that she seemed so happy to hang out with him. He felt permanently on autopilot in comparison with her, and half asleep. God knows, he pondered gloomily, what I can possibly offer her.

'This ghastly kids TV over here,' she would begin. 'I mean, do I need middle-aged women in romper suits and clown make-up gurning at my daughter before breakfast? As for their gross, pudgy men friends in ill-judged sweaters, well they are grotesque!'

Tom laughed. It was the way she hissed *sweaters*.

'I mean, I don't want to be a visual snob, but those sets and costumes are toxic. Why do they assume that kids can only engage with primary colours? And your BBC is the worst offender, piously promoting books and the importance of imagination on its children's channels when everyone knows that television is inimical to both. It's all so bogus . . . and as for those fat little guys wrapped in nasty-coloured fuzz. Yuck!'

'Tweenies? Fimbles? Teletubbies?' ventured Tom cautiously.

'Well, they're all the same – cheap live action and totally vile. Have you seen that gorgeous Japanese cartoon?'

Needless to say he hadn't, but thought instantly that he must.

On the evenings when Jeanette was out and Seamus was asleep, Tom read the stories Rose had given to him. Topping up his wine and kicking off his shoes, he would plunge excitedly into the entrancing and, to him, brand new world. He started with the ones Rose had starred before moving eagerly on to the others. It was a private indulgence but not in any way illicit, and each story gave him a burst of pleasure. He felt as though he were unwrapping and sucking brightly coloured sweets – sour fruit chews, maybe – and for days afterwards, the characters and their situations would buzz around in his mind like fizzy little depth-charges.

Tom's friendship with Rose and Esme was comfortably circumscribed by Queen's Park, pushchairs and the length of Thursday afternoons. They fell into a pattern of buying cappuccinos and cake before drifting over to the sandpit via the black-rubber baby swings. Rose rarely mentioned her partner, and although Tom said 'we' from time to time, he didn't discuss his wife much either. Tom's job was so relentlessly people-centred that he found it restorative to be with someone who would rather discuss stories and pictures than real life. He did reveal to Jeanette though, how much he liked Rose and Esme, and she seemed pleased that he'd found a child the same age for Seamus to hang out with. She didn't want to engage with the detail of it, though, and pretty soon interrupted him to enthuse about the new gym she'd joined. Jeanette had always been toned and fit, and when they made love these days, Tom felt a bit flabby by comparison.

On the Saturday of the bank holiday weekend, Jeanette, ostensibly finishing off some odds and ends at work, was in fact seeing and fucking a pre-marriage beau, no holes barred, no recriminations, short, sweaty and satisfying. Tom, meanwhile, was getting the car packed up for a trip to Devon. It was his favourite county and, uncharacteristically, he'd insisted on this break, although there did seem to be an inordinate amount of stuff to take. He parked Seamus in his high chair. It was now twelve-thirty and if Jeanette didn't get back soon there'd be little point in going. He'd feed the baby, make them some sandwiches for the drive and then they could leave. He was pretty confident that Jeanette would come flying in any minute, looking wonderful, and as usual he would instantly forgive her.

'Okay, let's go.'

'This minute?'

'Why not?'

That was one of the many things he loved about her. She travelled light and could turn on a sixpence. Jeanette was always on the move, which could be tiring, but there were never any hold-ups over select-ing outfits or fiddling about with accessories. She did expend a lot of energy on the gym, shopping and her appearance generally, but at the same time never seemed remotely weighed down by traditional women's clobber. Before they'd had Seamus, they'd decide to go off somewhere and she'd be out of the door while Tom was still planning how to get there. She would go away this weekend with just her handbag if she felt like it.

The phone rang and it was Jeanette. She was

sounding breathless at work rather than hurtling radiant through the front door as he'd hoped, having called him on her mobile as she ran up the path, pretending she was still miles away, which she sometimes did as a joke.

'Look, hon. I know it's got a bit late, but I'm almost through here now. Do you think you could pick me up from the tube in, say, forty minutes?'

Tom sighed. 'Fine. Don't be any later, though, sweetheart, please. Did you get the toothpaste for Seamus?'

There was a pause.

'Damn, Tom, I haven't had a moment. Any chance you could do it?'

Tom sighed again. He could feel his precious longed-for break slipping away.

'Yup, no problem. I can pick some up on the way. See you in a bit.'

Jeanette snapped her phone shut and winked at the spent man on the floor. 'Sorry about that. Just squaring hubby.'

Tom knew routine was important for babies, not to mention clean teeth every night. As a doctor, it just didn't bear thinking about, your kids needing fillings because you hadn't been arsed to brush their teeth properly, and a dentist mate he'd spoken to had been pretty clear that there was way too much fluoride for babies in grown-up toothpaste. He threw everything into the boot with these concerns swirling round his head and planted Seamus in his car seat with a board book to look at. He'd got hotter on books and visual stimulation, he realised, since meeting Rose. Jeanette's laughter rang in his ears. 'Tom, I know books and all that are important, but he's only one and a half!' She was probably right. Seamus would peak at ten years old and then swerve off the rails.

They would probably need cash, as well. Jeanette never had any. Tom reckoned that with luck he could park on the yellow line in the bendy lane off the main road and dash across to the cashpoint before picking up the toothpaste. Seamus was already heavy-lidded in the back. The car would certainly send him to sleep, which would have been perfect if they'd been speeding towards Devon. It was less than ideal when he had to be scooped like a sleepy small oyster out of his car seat, slopped into his buggy and dragged round an overlit chemist. Tom fought down his irritation. Never mind.

Jeanette was squirming into her designer jeans, zipping them up with difficulty. Her cheeks, flushed and post-orgasmic, would subside on the tube.

'Gottago, babe.' She pulled the boy to his feet. 'We should maybe leave by the fire door then I won't have to deal with the ancient security dweeb.'

The lad felt slightly thrown; not used, exactly, just a bit hurried along. He'd been hoping for something else – conversation, maybe; lunch, even? He wasn't sure exactly what it was that he craved, so he touched

Jeanette's neck to find out, but she shrugged him off, busily adjusting her T-shirt. She didn't have her own office, so on her way out carefully checked that they'd left nothing obviously out of place that could alert her colleagues to a weekend presence.

Tom spotted a gap that looked just about big enough and checked the car seat in his mirror. Predictably Seamus was now fast asleep. Still irked by Jeanette's inability to pull her weight, Tom completely misjudged the angle and the parked car ended up with its boot protruding way out into the road. Perhaps it didn't matter too much, as it was only going to be for a minute or two. Out of the car, the extent of his ineptitude became clear and he toyed with parking it better, but it just seemed too much of a performance. Keeping one eye on the car and sleeping baby he nipped across the road and joined the queue for the cashpoint. When there was only one person in front of him, a greasy youth with multiple cards pressing the buttons very deliberately and seeming to need each service more than once, Tom thought he heard someone call his name and looked over his shoulder. To his delight, Rose was crossing the road towards him with Esme in the pushchair being pushed by an older, bigger woman. A friend, maybe? An aunt or neighbour?

'Hi Tom! Good to see you. Meet my partner Liz.'

Tom was amazed and the naughty twinkle in Rose's eyes suggested she knew that he was thrown. Thankfully the scrofulous youth was finally through. Tom fished for his wallet, mind somersaulting, and then looked up and held out his hand.

'Hi, Liz. How nice to meet you. D'you mind if I . . .' He gestured at the machine.

The kids behind him in the queue were snogging so comprehensively that they hadn't noticed the short hiatus. Rose grinned.

'Go ahead, honey. We're in no rush.'

Tom got his money as Liz and Rose wandered to the back of the queue, which was now five or six deep. Rose made drinking gestures at Tom and pointed at the Starbucks just across the road. Tom looked at his watch and then across at Seamus fast asleep. Why not? He'd skip the toothpaste trauma, Seamus could stay asleep, he should still be able to pick Jeanette up on time, and a hit of frothy coffee with these two before his long drive would be fun. Besides, he was intrigued by the Liz factor and would welcome a bit more exposure to her. Was she good enough for his Rose? Who was Esme's dad, then? Well, he couldn't broach that one cold out here on the edge of the Kilburn High Road, that was for sure.

'Yeah, great. Could you get us takeaways? Then I could watch out for traffic wardens and keep an eye on Seamus.'

Rose followed his gesture, saw the car, and smiled. 'Wild parking, Tom!' On the way to Starbucks, she peeked through the car window at the sleeping boy, waved a slim wrist in the air to reassure Tom that Seamus was still okay, and danced off to get their coffees.

Tom went over to wait with Liz. Esme, unusually for her, was sunk in thought.

'She is quite extraordinarily pretty,' Tom said, meaning it as well as knowing it was a good way in.

Liz touched Esme's head lightly. 'We were very lucky. Rose was getting on, as it were, when we got together, and it seemed odd to rush into this when we were both coming out of other long relationships, but we decided to go for it anyway and it's turned out brilliantly. Rose's previous girlfriend, Laurie, was like a child herself, really. She needed a lot of looking after and Rose could never have had a baby with her, I don't think; and I had never wanted physically to have a child . . . well, not in the way Rose did. I still can't believe what I would have missed out on, though, by not being a parent. It's quite . . .' she searched for a word, forehead wrinkled up.

'Dazzling?' supplied Tom, confused by his own presumption.

Liz thought about it carefully and then smiled. 'Yes. Dazzling. That's precisely what it is. I'm dazzled by Esme. We both are, pretty much non-stop, I'd say. She is dazzling and just such an enchanting addition to our lives.'

Liz's whole face cracked in half and lit up unexpectedly when she smiled. She had lovely teeth, but she wasn't pretty or beautiful. Not at all. In fact she was quite grave in repose, but the smile definitely set her apart. So that was okay, Tom supposed. Jeanette was a bit dismissive of gay women on the whole. Dykes. Lezzers. He frowned. It didn't seem the right nomenclature for these two, somehow, although that, incontrovertibly, was what they were.

He glanced across at Seamus and the car again. All fine. As Rose dodged dangerously through the traffic with the coffees, the sun came out and Liz bent down to loosen Esme's funny little jacket. Tom momentarily felt light-headed, but couldn't work out why. He'd eaten that morning, wasn't more stressed than usual, had shared Seamus's cold a while ago now, so it wasn't that. Could it conceivably be contentment? Well-being? After all, an exotic woman had bought him a coffee and another woman with a lovely smile was standing beside him, happy with the description he'd selected for her experience of being a parent. In addition he had a dear little sleeping son, was off to the country with his wife and could forget about work for a couple of days.

Tom hitched his bum over a railing and carefully eased the lid off his coffee, keen to avoid sloppage on his clean holiday shirt. Licking the frothy chocolate powder off the underside and lobbing it into a nearby bin, he jauntily raised the brown paper cup.

'Cheers, m'dears.'

Esme picked up on it below him and started

chuntering quietly to herself, 'Cheers, cheers, cheers.'

They all smiled and Liz kissed Rose gently on the cheek. 'Thanks for the coffee, sweetheart. What a good thought that was.'

'The venue leaves something to be desired,' replied Rose. 'Carbon monoxide avenue.'

Liz winked at Tom. 'Yanks. They can be so precious, don't you find? Always banging on about the quality of the air. Or wondering if the rocket is organic?'

'Well, do we want to mess up our baby's motor functions with salads drenched in nerve-gas pesticides?' enquired Rose loftily.

'I think that's a little over the top.'

As Liz remonstrated with her girlfriend, they were interrupted by the high-pitched wine of a car travelling at speed. A dirty white beaten-up BMW hurtled over the horizon and flew down the hill towards them. The car was clearly out of control and as soon as he saw it, Tom knew it was going too fast. The driver would never be able to negotiate the narrower second half of the road where they were standing, which in addition had a slight kink in it. A wheel hit the kerb, bounced against a metal bollard and ploughed into the back of Tom's car with a splintering crash and thump. In the distance, almost on cue, there was the sound of sirens.

No one got out of the car and no one moved. No one spoke either, although Tom could see a chubby youth slumped over the steering wheel. His view of Seamus was blocked, but what he could see was that the crashed car had penetrated the boot and its bonnet was now thrust well up into the back seat area of his car. The BMW had buggered his car, raped it. That's what it looked like. Tom stared, confused, at a dark-skinned woman with orangey lipstick and a bad wig. She was wearing white thigh-boots and was carrying a plastic bag from Dixon's.

Tom touched her arm. 'My son is in that car.'

The woman shook her head. 'Well, he was driving much too fast, wasn't he?'

Rose took Tom's hand while still holding firmly onto Esme's pushchair. Tom's brain seemed frozen. I'm still connected to something, he thought. Rose is holding my hand. He took a shaky step forward into the road towards the accident.

'No.' Rose's voice was high and sharp. He'd never heard it like that before. 'No, Tom. Let Liz go see.'

Tom looked at her and shook his head, maddened. He felt that there was an insect flying around inside his skull, buzzing between his ears. He looked at Rose. 'What about his toothpaste?' He started to cross the road again. 'I have to go, Rose, as Seamus might be frightened, poor chap. It was a helluva bang.'

Rose let go of the pushchair, and the orange-lipstick woman instinctively gripped the handle in her place. Rose hurled herself at Tom, wrapped both tiny arms round his waist and physically prevented him from crossing the road. She buried her face in his stomach and turned him away from the accident. Then she slid her face sideways so she could see Liz on the other side of the street past Tom's waist. She'll feel my spare tyre, thought Tom. I don't want her to know I'm a bit lardy. I don't want her to be disgusted by me. I really like her. I want her to be my friend.

Liz pushed her way back out through the crowd that had gathered round the cars. Her face had gone white-grey and she thought that she was going to faint. Dazed and nauseous, she somehow managed to identify the little balloon of Rose's face across the road through the shimmering haze of her shock. Shaking her head she swayed against a lamppost, sliding slowly into a gritty puddle that was filled with floating crisp-packets.

For the rest of that day, passers-by on various errands stopped and stood around awkwardly while the predatory car was winched off its victim. Then people started to bring bouquets. They laid them carefully on the pavement and tied them to the nearby railings, their heels grinding on shattered glass and slivers of metal. Two self-important small girls carefully deposited a pink teddy bear with a note as an older lad and his grandmother crossed themselves. Everyone hoped that by paying their respects, and by acknowledging what had occurred that morning, they might somehow ward off anything similar that could even now be entering their own orbits and hurtling towards them or their families.

234